RAZE VS THE WOLF

Raze vs The Wolf

Book three in the Raze Warfare series

SHELLEY CASS

A trigger warning for readers:
there are emotional and mental abuse scenes,
as well as violent scenes in this novel.

For those who are a work in progress.
For those who are willing to be Raze in their own way.
For those who know that love is love, and how greatly the world needs it.

RECEIVE YOUR EXTRA RAZE WARFARE CHAPTER WHEN YOU SIGN UP FOR SHELLEY CASS' VIP LIST. GET YOUR BONUS HERE:

shelleycass.com/coming-soon-02

LINK TO FREE VIP READER GIFT

Razes, Razes, the Wolf's prey.
Razes, Razes, all betrayed …

| 1 |

One

"Mister Lake."

That's all Chef Narkon had to say.

The implications behind needing to stay back for a quiet word with the chef were never good ones.

The other apprentices, neat and tidy in their black server uniforms, or their crisp whites for the kitchen, cast sympathetic glances at Kiddo as they filed past to leave for the day.

Kiddo stayed at his counter, straight faced and straight backed. He was very aware of the tear in the seam at his shoulder, and that at least two black buttons on the double breasted jacket were hanging loose.

Chef Narkon, hands clasped behind his back, moved through the trail of promising young culinary artists and waiters as they exited the shiny, ordered kitchen. He was like a shark splitting streams of terrified fish as they hurried by.

He came to a stop at Kiddo's immaculate counter as the last apprentice let the swinging doors close.

"Chef," Kiddo acknowledged his superior steadily. He was

making a strong effort to maintain his flawless posture. Slouching wasn't tolerated.

Narkon's eyes roamed over the tear and the buttons. They stopped on Kiddo's jaw.

"You were late to the practical."

Kiddo's jaw was still throbbing from where the Hunter had managed to get a punch in earlier.

Kid had fallen for the oldest trick in the book – being lured off track by the sight of a couple of snatchers stalking a child down an alley.

Turned out the child; a little girl who must have been younger than ten, was a play acting snatcher herself. The Hunter had closed in on Kiddo from behind, grabbing for, and ultimately tearing, his white coat.

Stupid, stupid, stupid.

Kiddo had wanted to be prepared. He'd already been wearing his uniform on the way to the assessment.

Luckily, he'd also been carrying his roll of knives, and only Kiddo's quick hustle to slip a knife free had helped him to slash his way out of that whole mess.

Of course, after chopping through all that, the blade would need some serious sterilising before it could be used again.

The baby snatcher girl had assumed the mean look of someone who might just as easily slash her way through Kiddo herself, but he'd let her bolt by him and had accepted her kick to his shins in passing.

He'd dusted her dirty shoe print from his black trousers, and had high-tailed his way to the academy restaurant with no time to worry about the other imperfections to his uniform. It was incredible that his whites weren't also blemished by any reds.

"I was right on time for the practical to begin, Chef," Kiddo answered.

Narkon regarded him coolly. "Right on time, is already too late."

Too late to make a good impression, too late to help the team set up, too late to show you really cared about the job.

Kiddo kept himself from fidgeting. He dipped his head curtly in acceptance.

"A ruffian who doesn't take pride in his own presentation is also not going to make it far in this environment," Narkon went on. "You need to change your ways."

The tip of the scar on the side of Kiddo's scalp showed from under his cap. Last week he'd been limping. The week before it had been bloody knuckles and a swollen shut eye. The colours were still blooming around his eye socket even now, to compliment the bruise he was working up on that jaw.

For someone so reserved and on edge, Kiddo still didn't have the air of a victim. So he probably seemed like he simply picked too many fights.

"Your fellows also very obviously try to please and help you, following your lead and pandering to you. But you keep them at arm's length," Narkon said.

Oh dear. A tardy, sloppy, poor team player with aggression issues. Kiddo wouldn't hire himself at this rate.

"Chef," Kiddo said with a sigh of resignation. "Did I fail this practical?"

Narkon pursed his lips. He somehow drew himself up to be taller and even more formidable.

He was a highly respected French chef, a master across all of Europe. And here he was, giving his time to train promising new chefs at a prestigious university, while coming across a tardy, sloppy, unhelpful 'ruffian' who'd been meant to stick to cookery classes.

"You did not fail."

The way he said it made it sound like Kiddo actually really had failed, even if not academically.

"… Great," Kiddo replied after a pause. "Then I'll be out of your way. That was my last assessment."

Narkon moved to fold his arms now. "That is why I am disappointed."

Kiddo frowned.

"You shone so brightly in your early courses that your trainers convinced *me* to accept you into this specialty intensive program. You had the opportunity to be pitted against skilled peers, you gained experiences you shouldn't have gained for years."

Most of those advances had happened almost against Kid's will.

Kiddo had found himself being passed from level to level by well-meaning and pleased trainers. They'd always broken the news to him, that they'd granted him such favours, when it was too late to politely decline. He'd been signed up for competitions. Tested. Awarded. And recommended on as if it were a gift.

"You passed each of your assessments with creative flair,

produced quality dishes, and performed spectacularly under pressure," Narkon threw the words at Kid as if they were accusations rather than compliments.

"However, you're choosing to leave now, with only general qualifications."

Narkon shook his head, frustrated.

"It's lazy, and it's selfish, to throw away your chance for a life in superior kitchens, for customers who can appreciate fine dining, when this is a *dream* for others!"

Kiddo waited a moment to see if anything else was coming.

Narkon was also waiting – for an apology or an epiphany, or something.

"Thank you for your time, and your ..." Kiddo considered his words. "Truly flattering and galvanising feedback." Arrogant and insulting, more like. "However, I have my own diner waiting for me. And that has been *my* dream. I appreciate your help in getting me there, and will proudly display the certificate with your signature on it when it arrives."

"You're wasting your talent," Narkon stated, point-blank. "On diner food and diner clients." He was genuinely incredulous.

"My first fast tracked, and sincerely brilliant student ... wants to serve burgers and fries." He said it with unveiled disapproval. "You could take on real prestige and a real challenge!"

Kiddo slowly reached for his cap and dragged it from his head. He placed it neatly on top of his roll of knives, and scooped them up to leave.

"Chef, I would hate to waste my life serving people with high tastes and full wallets," Kiddo said carefully. "Reaching their type of culinary expectations isn't my style of challenge."

He neglected to say that, too often, he had found these exact kinds of people, with great demands, high tastes and full wallets, to be his direct opponents in the underworld.

"Burgers and fries clients are my sort of people," Kiddo added.

Narkon's brow was furrowed in consternation. As if he simply could not understand how he had failed to get through to this student.

This tardy, sloppy, unhelpful, lazy, selfish student, who – with that list in mind – should have been exited swiftly from the university, rather than being head hunted by a top chef for a glitzy future.

"You would prefer a life of fist fights and generic dishes?"

Kiddo's gaze was almost sympathetic. "Chef, I understand that my choices appear disappointing to you. But, I wonder myself, why you are retiring at the end of this year. You are fifty years old, at the top of your game, and you decided to leave your own kitchens, your own travels and prestigious clients, to try your hand at teaching. Even that couldn't enthuse you, and you are wrapping up after this stint."

Kiddo stepped away from the counter.

"It's almost as if *you* are unhappy with this type of challenge too."

Narkon was silent. Stony.

"I do thank you Chef," Kiddo told him. "I'm grateful to have had this experience."

He left the kitchen.

| 2 |

Two

"Kid's back!"

"Kiddo! Did you pass?"

"What did that old Narkon say this time?"

Kiddo ducked under the roller door to the ground level of the gang's warehouse complex.

"Jeffrey, you have no idea how to play dead," Dom admonished the oldest recruit dryly. "No wonder Flip never passed you for international missions."

Nevertheless, Dom turned with an enthusiastic grin for Kiddo.

Then his grin faded as Kiddo stepped into the light.

"Is that another bruise?" Sparks was wiping her hands on a rag. She tossed it to one of her apprentices, and crossed to meet Kiddo and Dom in the open space between the garage and training areas.

"Got jumped on the way to the practical," Kiddo grimaced.

Jeffrey and the other recruits made concerned, very much alive noises from their prone positions.

"Lucky you're good at stitching," Sparks replied unhappily.

She moved to pick at the tear in his white coat, but stopped when she realised her hands were still greasy.

Kid grabbed her hands with a small smile and pulled her so that her arms encircled his waist.

"I passed. I won't be wearing this get-up again."

Dom was grim faced. "I need to go back to escorting you, like the school days."

"No fear. I tested the sharpness of my best knife on them. Only let one get away," Kiddo reassured him.

"Why'd you let one escape?" Jeffrey called out. His lung capacity was really superb for a corpse.

"It was a baby snatcher," Kiddo answered darkly. "I hope it's not a new trend while they're trying so desperately to rebuild here."

"Bleh," Jeffrey angled himself up on his elbows. "Raze has been seeing one around too. He said they might start to use younger children to throw us off, cos we're less likely to want to hurt them."

"Lordy, lordy," Dom said sardonically. "He listens."

"And it's true," Kiddo agreed. "I couldn't face up to taking on such a small urchin."

Sparks released Kiddo and smacked him on the butt. "Forget it for this evening. You should be celebrating. And you won't be as easy to trace now that your schedule won't be so obvious."

Kiddo had been the one gang member who'd had to follow an obvious and entirely routine timetable during his studies. The others were mostly covert or erratic in their movements, but he had been a Hunter magnet for months.

"He'll be even more predictable," Dom negated glumly. "He'll be in the diner full time."

Sparks spanked Dom on the butt too, trying to snap him out of his mood. "And we'll be over here, just across the road, like we have been while he's been working it part time."

Dom sighed, and he had a weariness about him that had first begun when Yorak the Wolf had brought The Hunt into their lives.

After Yorak had found a way to infiltrate the gang's group chat, they had all braced for the worst. A technological or physical take down.

But it had never come.

They had waited, they had fortified, they had readied. But nothing further had happened.

It wasn't like he would bomb the place, when he wanted the Razes alive. But he hadn't tried to breach them either.

Even the small-scale, regular skirmishes and attempted snatchings were odd. They had never shown enough planning to do any real damage, when it would have been easy for the Wolf to coordinate something efficient and devastating.

Jingle was convinced it was to drive her mad.

Kiddo thought it was because Yorak was still happy to play his long game as he established himself.

And Dom was tired.

Being part of a group for once, and in charge of many people, had made the stakes higher. He might not be getting hurt in the usual ways or as often anymore, but he was hurting in new ways.

While The Hunt hounded them, the Raze gang had had to keep up their fight against the snatchers. And Flip and the others had gone back to work so well, that there were now one hundred and seventy eight bases left around the world. Seventeen capital headquarters down.

It was Dom's job to get recruits ready to help Flip against the snatcher civilisations, and to select those who could go after The Hunt. Sometimes it seemed the Hunters and Razes were killing each other off as quickly as they could be trained. And while recruits were only chosen from those keen applicants who were of an acceptable age and level of talent, who purposefully came to join the cause – Dom was still the one who got to know and to lose them.

Sparks leaned around Dom, seeing his exhaustion. "Hey everyone," she called to his recruits. "Take a break."

"How much more of a break do they need?" Dom asked incredulously. "They're laying down."

"Yayyyyyy," Jeffrey and the others lolled about. "We're aliiiiiiiiiveeee."

Dom rolled his eyes.

"I've got to keep going," Sparks informed him. "I have a call coming up with Trix about our grenade updates. So it's your job to make sure Kiddo feels properly celebrated before his shift starts at the diner tonight."

Kiddo tilted his head and put on his best 'please?' expression.

Dom rubbed his face. "Right, right, right. I can do that."

He eyed Kiddo with returning energy.

"First thing is to get that jacket off."

| 3 |

Three

Kiddo breathed into his hands as he crossed the road toward the inviting lights of 'Kid's Place'.

A line stretched out from The Lair, and the music was pumping, so the diner opposite would be busy for hours tonight.

The diner front was all windows, so he could see that most of the booths were already full.

The bell on the door jingled, and he crossed to lean against the counter, beside where Pash was swivelling lazily on a red stool.

"Hey pet," Pash greeted him. She sipped contentedly at a strawberry milkshake, scrolling through her socials.

Apparently a pink filtered snap of her milkshake, combined with the red toned diner aesthetic, had already accumulated over a thousand 'hearts' before she'd finished drinking. And the number was rising.

"Heard you passed," she swivelled back his way.

Aside from posting to her expanding, loyal global fan base,

Pash would have been checking the gang's new, air-tight group chat. It was a place for counting losses and successes.

Someone else bounced up behind Kiddo and threw warm arms around him before he could answer.

"Congratulations Kiddo!" a playful voice sang happily.

"Thanks Teddy," Kiddo grinned, reaching back to hug her too.

Her round face beamed up at him, and her innocent, unrestricted happiness for his success at once made him feel lighter, as it usually did.

It was 'Kid's Place', but Teddy had become the heart of it since he had employed her.

"Want me to call you a taxi?" he asked. "It's getting darker earlier now."

Pash gave a final slurp.

"What do you think I'm here for?" Pash quirked a smile. "Apart from the milkshake."

"She's here for me," Teddy told Kid proudly, pointing her thumb into her chest. "Pash offers me a ride when she's free. She has all those followers, but I'm the one in her car."

Teddy was a hugger, a joyful soul, an equally grumpy soul, and beloved by the Razes.

Like many, one way or another she had heard of Hato's gang's mission. She had decided she wanted to help.

Not all people who wandered in from near or far to join Hato's gang were suited to be Razes. Sparks' apprentices were often rescues or street kids who wanted the hands-on experience, but couldn't afford it or sustain a normal job. Frazzle and Doctor Daleeah selected their trainees and staff from all over, especially because the applicants wanted to help the clinic's specific cause. While Kiddo hired the people who had too much heart to hurt anyone – and just the right amount of heart to feed them.

"You're lucky, Teddy," Kiddo grinned. "Pash normally gets chauffeured around, rather than doing the chauffeuring."

Teddy took off her apron. "She does it because it's for me."

Pash slipped down from her stool. "Damn straight, doll." She gave Kiddo a kiss on the cheek before linking arms with Teddy.

It wasn't because Teddy had Down Syndrome that everyone felt protective of her. It was because she was Teddy. The sweetest, most brutally honest, and most caring soul, who could cheer up the most miserable client off the streets.

Even Hato got all soft around her. He treated her like she was a cute little kitten in need of mollycoddling.

And, for Hato, she acted as if she wasn't perfectly capable of running the entire diner by herself. Just to make him feel needed when he came in.

Kiddo greeted the other servers as they collected or delivered dishes. He alternated between taking and making orders – relishing the freedom of being the owner and manager of his own kitchen.

Wasting his talents, indeed.

"Well, this is … nice."

Kiddo's heart froze for a moment.

His eyes flicked to the stool Pash had occupied earlier.

He closed the till a little too firmly.

"Chef Narkon."

The head chef was so out of place. So unexpected in this environment.

Narkon cast his eyes over the clientele.

There were a mix of grungy pre-clubbers, off duty and overly loud Razes, street kids, families who had just stopped by for a meal, and people who looked as if they had been battling various demons for years. Homelessness, poverty, drugs, whatever it was.

They either kept to themselves in the safety of their booth, or laughed with others they'd come to know in the diner. All enjoying the full plate in front of them.

For the mix of people, the scene had a positive vibe.

Only Narkon was truly odd here.

His hands were folded neatly on the countertop. His jacket was too formal. His slick hair, for once not covered by a superior sized white hat, was just too carefully combed back.

"To what do I owe the honour?" Kiddo asked. Trying not to sound unwelcoming. Or flabbergasted.

"I came to see why you made such a choice."

Narkon's expression suggested he still wasn't finding any real answers that could possibly justify Kiddo's decision.

All he could see was a typical diner, with a generic menu, and with unusually mixed and boisterous patrons.

"Right, well," Kiddo grunted. "While you work it out, I'll get you tonight's special."

He would prefer to personally prepare this one, rather than staying out at the counter with Narkon.

He wasn't in the mood to be the respectful 'yes, Chef!' student now that he was finished with the course.

He left the orders and payments to the other staff, and prepared his finest dish for the day.

Narkon was still waiting patiently when Kiddo returned, setting the special on the counter.

Narkon blinked down at it. And then he cracked a smile.

A stiff and almost unyielding smile, but a smile all the same.

"A burger and fries."

Not even a sliver of decorative garnish.

Kiddo stared back unwaveringly. "Correct. Please enjoy."

Narkon surprised Kiddo; opting to lift the burger from the plate, rather than going for the napkin wrapped cutlery beside his elbow.

"I'm just not seeing it," Narkon commented. "I'm really not seeing the reason."

Kiddo nodded. "I know you're not seeing it. I was sure you wouldn't."

Narkon's brow furrowed. It was the first time that an underling of his had made him feel that *he* was the one at risk of failing here.

"I appreciate that you went out of your way to try. It really wasn't necessary," Kiddo went on.

"See ya, Kid," a weathered, rugged patron waved at Kiddo before exiting. "Thanks."

"G'night," Kid answered in farewell.

Narkon chewed a small mouthful, eyeing Kiddo thoughtfully.

At this rate, the chef would be eating the burger all night.

Narkon swallowed.

"That man didn't pay."

Kiddo shrugged, unbothered. "You're right."

Narkon was chewing again, as refined as if he were sampling a gourmet hors d'oeuvre.

He observed an animated family with six squalling kids, some lively young clubbers, and the group of cheerful Raze recruits each pay for their meal, while another four people thanked Kiddo and left without visiting the till.

"That is the longest lasting burger I've ever seen," Kiddo at last remarked wryly. He could feel Narkon's watchful eyes.

"I'm savouring it. It's quite good."

Kiddo didn't say anything. He just waited to find out what Narkon thought *wasn't* good. The chef took the critiquing side of his job very seriously at all times.

"However," Narkon went on after another mouthful.

There it was. It set Kiddo's aching jaw on edge.

"I feel it is my responsibility to warn you that your prices are too low and that a tab system is not a good idea at all."

Kiddo folded his arms.

"It's not a tab system."

It was the first time that Kiddo had seen a 'huh?' expression cross the unshakable Narkon's face.

"If they can pay, they pay. If they can't, they don't."

Both Kid's Place and Frazzle's medical clinic did mostly scrape by on their own. The clinic also did well for donations. But all of the businesses under Hato's wing shared from a collective pool. There was the unofficial funding of the Raze gang's missions, the contract work that Sparks and Jingle did, and the earnings of The Lair.

Narkon's mouth hung open. But he didn't put the final bite of burger in there to fill it up.

"How in the world does that work? Your diner counts on an honesty system?" Narkon asked in bewilderment.

"Yes. And my gang and I also know the people in this area well. We're good at being able to tell who is genuine."

Narkon balked.

It might have been the word 'gang' that threw him.

Or the word 'honesty' when applied to running a business.

"That is a terrible business model!" Narkon spluttered.

Of course it was.

Kiddo nodded. "But, seeing as I can afford to run it like that, it's a good life model."

It was a utopian dream. Even before Kiddo had started his most basic introductory business course, he'd known their set up would be a commercial disaster in any other situation, and in the eyes of any other entrepreneur.

"I don't see *how* you've been able to afford to run it like that," Narkon stated. "You have to know you won't be able to survive like this for long."

Kiddo had started to wipe down the counter. The dinner rush was over. The night owls would be transitioning in for the quieter part of the evening soon.

"It's been working so far. I opened this place before I transferred into your specialty training."

Narkon considered that.

It was over nine months then.

"Mister Lake," Narkon started.

"Kiddo," Kid corrected.

"You mentioned a gang," the chef stated bluntly. "Getting help from the wrong people ..."

"Now *that* would be a bad idea," Kiddo agreed. "Luckily my business is tied to the mechanic, the club, and the community medical centre all thriving across the road. All above board." No need to mention the unofficial extras.

Narkon was silent. He took his final bite.

He was somewhat impressed. This young man was barely twenty, yet perhaps he was quite shrewd, despite his youth and impractical idealism.

"It's getting late," Kiddo mentioned, with a not so indirect hint.

"I'm a chef. I am used to odd hours."

"You've let the rest of the meal get cold. You're not really a burger and fries person, after all," Kiddo stated.

Narkon nearly snorted.

Earlier, Kiddo had announced that burgers and fries types of people were his kinds of people. So Narkon wasn't in that category.

Honestly, most people in the food business fell over themselves for a moment of the master chef's attention. This young man instead seemed bothered and inconvenienced by it.

Narkon surveyed the quietening diner again.

There were a few loners left after the rush. They were scattered about, huddled over their coffees as if those cups were the warmest things they would see for the night. Or ever.

An old woman had a magazine open at her booth. For some reason, she had a dainty china teacup instead of the usual white mug. Her jumper was horrifically patterned, with an equally awful peacock pin. But she seemed so cosy.

Narkon was beginning to guess why Kiddo had been disappointed that Narkon 'couldn't see it'.

It was because he hadn't been seeing the people.

Or what a place like this could give to people.

Narkon felt a sense of heaviness when he realised it had been decades since he had really seen or felt any affinity for the clients he had served.

"Hey Kid!"

A couple of adolescents who had the look of the street about them – the kind you might be scared to run into at first sight – ducked inside then.

"Yo, Kiddo," the male called gaily, scooting into a booth. "Boss man says to tell your boyfriend to back off. We really don't deal in drugs as a side hustle anymore."

Kiddo groaned. "You don't deal in subtlety either, Beef Cake! Miss Dorris is trying to read her magazine."

Beef Cake?

The female, who had settled in opposite Beef Cake, gave him a kick.

"Miss Dorris is Raze's nanna," she hissed.

"But … Raze is so white?" Beef Cake whispered much too loudly back.

The girl reached over and slapped the back of Beef Cake's head. "If Raze says she's his nan, that's what she is."

"Yeah, alright," Beef Cake agreed. "Sorry Miss Dorris! But Raze is making us nervous with all his check-ups. Boss man Sora's getting annoyed."

Miss Dorris actually now appeared to be nodding over her magazine. She might have been snoozing the whole time.

Kiddo grabbed some mugs and a coffee pot, circling the counter and filling the cups for the two young hoodlums.

"Then keep up the good work going semi straight with the cars," Kid told them. "And Raze'll get bored and go away."

"He should check up on the Dire Gang across the tracks," Beef Cake complained. "They're way worse than us. Bunch of crazy bikers."

"You don't think he checks on your rivals too?" Kid asked.

"I don't mind if he keeps visiting," the girl shrugged. "He's so pretty."

Kiddo leaned in as if he was confiding in her. "He is. Why don't you join the Raze gang so you can see him all the time?"

She blushed, her eyes brightening. "As if you think I'm Raze material," she scoffed. She was trying to laugh it off, and to get Kiddo's reassurance all at once.

"In this diner I sometimes get to see who might have potential," Kiddo straightened, no longer teasing. "I could recommend you."

"What about me?" Beef Cake burst out.

"Mmm," Kiddo cocked his head. "I'm less sure on that one. I'll keep watching."

Beef Cake took that on the chin, nodding his ascent rather than being put out.

"Alright, man," Beef Cake announced. "Boss would be so proud."

"Although, Sora would hate to lose either of us to Seethe," the girl smirked. "Seethe used to steal our best cars. And then he stole Sparks for your gang."

When Kiddo came back, he pointedly slid Narkon's plate of cold fries away to hand it to a waiter.

"See, I happen to know *they* can pay," Kiddo informed the chef. "And I am certain that you can pay, too."

"Who is Raze? And what are the Raze gang?" Narkon asked inquisitively.

Narkon had come to force his student to see the light. Instead, he was the one starting to see something glimmering faintly here. His interest was piqued.

"My boyfriend. And something that the general public don't have to worry about."

Narkon took out his wallet.

"Aren't you going to tell me to please come again?" the chef asked.

"No." Kiddo deadpanned. "Please enjoy the rest of your night."

He swiped Narkon's card and handed it back.

As if that was that.

| 4 |

Four

"It's so late," Kiddo reprimanded Sparks. "Don't fall asleep in there. We'd never recover you amongst the bubbles."

He'd found her in the bath, and her eyes had indeed been closed.

She blinked up at him and smiled.

"One down."

"Hmm?"

"You're home. Now waiting on Dom."

Kid was even later than hoped, after taking Miss Dorris home in her ancient car.

Kiddo sat down on the tiles, leaning his arm and chin on the tub.

"As of tomorrow, my life contains more sleep-ins ahead. Yours doesn't," he said. "You shouldn't wait up for us."

"I bet Raff was the one who told you I was still up," Sparks laughed. "And I bet you didn't scold him for having a late night."

Raff had indeed been reading the paper at the dining table when Kiddo had got home. He'd had a sandwich ready for

Kiddo to midnight snack on, with another two cling-wrapped plates waiting for when Hato finished up at the club and Dom returned from patrol.

"Raff's not under heavy cars all day ... or playing with potent weapons."

Of course, Raff's job as a housekeeper for an ever expanding household was possibly just as perilous.

Kiddo flicked some water at her. "Why have you really started waiting up? Or did things take a while on the call to Trix?"

Sparks grimaced and shook her head. "No, Trix and I are making great progress. I just wanted to be sure the two of you got in. Especially seeing as you're finding yourself in constant brawls, and Dom can't sit still. He keeps doing whatever extra patrols he can on his own, and then comes home exhausted, with headaches and with his mind elsewhere entirely."

Kiddo nodded. "Three past recruits did die on Flip's last base take-down," he said soberly. "Considering the scale of the task, those statistics are nothing. But to us, and to Dom, they're everything."

"He's working the new recruits incredibly hard," Sparks agreed. "He's pushing them to think harder, to lead more often, and to take more calculated risks. And they adore him for it, because they know he's just worried. But I think he's going it alone so often in his spare time too, because he's feeling sick about who he might send out and lose next."

Kiddo thought about it. He'd been too focused on surviving all of his own assessments and challenges in recent months. He had to turn his attention outward.

"Maybe Dom needs a break."

He reached for Sparks' arm and then for her towel, pulling her up from the water.

"Come on," he said, settling the towel around her warmly. "Quicklips and Seethe have just got back. Pash and Jingle are around. They'll be up for heading some patrols. And with classes done, all I've got are night shifts, so I'll have free days. I'll take care of cheering Dom up."

Hopefully that would lift some troubles from Sparks' shoulders too.

Sparks leaned her forehead against his chest, standing in the water.

"Have you noticed how Yorak doesn't even have to do anything, and he's still getting to us?" she questioned in a muffled voice, and Kiddo rubbed her shoulders under the towel in an effort to be reassuring.

"Jingle heard that he's been here in our city, moving in and out regularly without fear," Sparks shivered. "But he never does anything to provoke us, and she only finds out he was even here once he's had his fill of meetings and has moved on."

Jingle in particular was becoming increasingly agitated as she sought out the Wolf. She'd chased him out of the gang's security system, but she had not been able to breach The Hunt's own system in return. They only found out what Yorak was doing or where he was going when he chose to reveal himself.

Flip's Razes hadn't just suffered deaths on the job either. A few had been captured by Yorak's Hunt and sold on by snatchers as prizes for the elite. Every time Jingle had tracked down the sale, it had been too late for the gang to do more than take vengeance on the buyers who had done the damage. It was what Quicklips and Seethe had just returned from.

Start, Tiny, Velvet and Flip hardly made it home between jobs anymore.

And Hato worried for them all while his empire for the vulnerable grew.

Kiddo rubbed Sparks' back now. "Frazzle and Daleeah's wedding will bring us all back together in a few months," he said comfortingly. "It'll feel like normal."

"For a little while, at least," she sighed.

He hugged her harder and lifted her out of the bath.

"Get to bed soon, right?" he told her sternly.

She worked the hardest out of everybody, and that was saying something.

"Right. And you concoct some respite ideas for Dom."

"Right."

He took it to heart, and by the time Dom's chilled body was sliding into bed beside Kiddo's, Kid had it all organised. Seethe would run the next day's training, and Quicklips would lead the night.

"How's your head?" Kiddo whispered.

He rolled over to draw Dom in closer and to share his own body heat.

Dom didn't even try to seduce him with the usual tricks.

"Up in the clouds. And the clouds are thundering," Dom admitted. "Raff's sandwich didn't even help." His words were punctuated by an uncontrollable chatter from his teeth.

"Seethe's got you covered for tomorrow. You and I are going to sleep in. Then we're going to spend some quality time together."

Dom shivered against him. "Thank you. I think I need that."

Kiddo felt a pang in his heart and pulled the covers up higher around Dom's shoulders.

"How's your ..." Dom paused to try to recall where Kiddo's most recent bruise was. "How's your jaw?"

"I've been told it's defined. Quite aesthetic."

Dom let out a puff of air that would pass for a laugh. "Everything about you is aesthetic."

"Oh, it is," Kiddo agreed. "But it means more when you say it."

"Then you are aesthetic all over. So aesthetic that it hurts. It hurts so much that I love it."

Kiddo kissed Dom's cheekbone.

Dom went along prattling tiredly. "It's so nice that I'm safe with you. You love me. You are always helping me."

Kid smiled to himself.

"Get to sleep. You're delirious."

"Only a bit."

| 5 |

Five

Dom slept so late that Kiddo had already balanced the books and put in orders for The Lair, Kid's Place and Sparks' shop by the time Dom made it up to the library level.

Jingle's business dealings, Sparks' weapons and the medical compound were beyond him, but Kiddo still felt satisfied to be able to do the others.

"I slept through the start of date day," Dom shook his head blearily. "What a fun date I am."

He was a barefoot, sleepy masterpiece in blue jeans and a white tee.

Though Kiddo noticed that the t-shirt had become loose on the already slim waisted Dom, Kid grinned as Dom came to lean against his table. A hint of Kiddo's own aftershave, as well as mint toothpaste, told him Dom had made some effort to pull himself together already.

"You leaned right there on the first night that I met you," Kiddo told him.

The moment was captured like a photograph in Kiddo's

memory. Leather jacket, silvery moonlight, and a lotus tat-tooed finger, pointing against Kiddo's chest.

"How cocky I was," Dom snickered. "You weren't giving me enough attention from my spot on the window sill. I had to get right in front of you."

Kiddo leaned his chin in his hand. "You don't think you're so cocky anymore?" he teased.

Dom considered it. Taking the question seriously. "I'm still overly confident in my usual self," he admitted. "But I don't feel as much like my usual self as I would like right now."

Kiddo nodded thoughtfully. "That's alright," he said. "I'm confident in all versions of you."

Dom gave a half smile.

"But I feel like the current version of you, needs an easy day," Kiddo speculated.

"Oh no, I'm up for our quality time," Dom negated. "I can wield one hundred percent energy once I get going – just ask Jeffrey and co."

Kiddo tapped his chin. "Quality time doesn't always have to be action packed, you know. I'm going to give you the most average day you've ever had, and you're going to love it."

"Alright," Dom agreed with interest. "What normal thing shall we do first?"

"We'll grab you some shoes and a jacket to start with," Kiddo laughed. "And then we'll kiss Sparks good morning."

"I better hurry," Dom straightened. "There're only a few minutes of the morning left."

Sparks was under a bonnet, explaining something to her

apprentices as she pointed out a trouble spot in the car's workings with a torch.

But as soon as she realised they were there, she threw her arms around Dom's neck as if she had never been so delighted to see anybody before.

"The recruits have been complaining all morning," she informed him. "But they're in good hands."

"Raaaaazeee," Jeffrey's voice whined when he spotted the three of them on Spark's side of the ground level.

His arms were shaking as he fought to hold a chin-up. His higher vantage was likely thanks to a punishment, because the others were doing morose laps through an obstacle course of old tyres.

"Don't you love us anymore?" Jeffrey huffed and sweated. "Who would need a break from us?"

Dom and Kiddo meandered over. "I love you all too much," Dom professed. "It's wearing me out."

It came off as a frivolous joke, but Kiddo heard the ring of truth to it.

"You've got *me* to make up for it," Seethe scowled at Jeffrey. "And I have no such issues. So don't worry that I'll tire out."

Jeffrey whimpered.

"Now get back in line and keep up with the others," Seethe hissed. "Or we'll use you for the target on the shooting range."

Jeffrey dropped down with relief to dash away.

"You're so mean," Dom complimented Seethe, observing the obstacle course with appreciation.

"Yup," Seethe shrugged. "Where you both off to?"

"Second on the list is to walk and get food," Kiddo supplied.

Seethe nodded slowly. He eyed Dom. Probably noticing the looser than normal clothes and the dark circles under Dom's eyes too.

"Well I'm enjoying myself so far," Seethe drawled in a slightly less acidic tone than usual. "So I'll do tomorrow too."

Dom made to wave that suggestion away, but Kiddo cut him off.

"That's great. Thanks," Kid said appreciatively, tugging Dom toward the open roller doors.

They stepped out into the sun.

"Quicklips can make sure the recruits show their faces in all the right areas and keep up patrol tonight," Kiddo reassured Dom. "And Hato has Jingle and Pash for the club. Then with the idea of another free day ahead tomorrow, you can properly relax today."

Dom took a deep breath of fresh air. "Alright then, you're the boss."

They strolled at an easy pace through the streets, and Kiddo bought them terribly greasy, fried dim-sims as they passed a stall.

The oil seeped through the brown paper bags, and made their lips shinier with each gristly bite, but Dom grinned at the simple pleasure of it.

"This has got to be the unhealthiest food you've touched in months," Dom told Kiddo, finishing his last dim-sim with relish.

"Narkon definitely never asked us to prepare anything like it," Kiddo granted.

"And Raff always makes nutritious meals," Dom added. "While you, yourself aim to order the freshest you can get for Kid's Place."

Kiddo did have the classic diner dishes. But he also went out of his way to provide nourishing food. Wholesome meals that could help someone get through the coldest nights.

"Narkon visited the diner yesterday," Kiddo recounted, shaking his head.

"Wanted to see his high achiever one last time?" Dom enquired.

Kiddo snorted. "Wanted to tell his promising student off for mediocre choices."

"Wowee," Dom threw his paper bag in the trash and shoved his hands in his pockets.

"He thinks I have a bad business model, am a gangster and am in with the wrong crowd."

"Hmmm," Dom reflected. "Smart man. Very savvy."

Kid elbowed him. "He would prefer *I* smarten up by wasting my life in fancy kitchens."

"Yours is fancy."

"Yes, I think so."

Dom blinked when he recognised where they were.

"Are we paying a visit?" he asked in surprise.

They were near Miss Dorris' street.

"Your adopted grandmother has a cough that hasn't cleared up," Kiddo answered. "Last night when I dropped her off I told her we would come back and take her to the clinic."

At some point Dom had become good friends with the little, addled old lady whose car he had borrowed once upon a time. Such good friends, that she had even come to remember him, and had decided to make him one of her own.

"Number three on the average date day list, is to go to a check-up."

Kiddo didn't just mean for Miss Dorris.

"You're so thoughtful," Dom replied warmly. "A very fulfilling way to spend our time."

He took the fire escape stairs instead of going through the apartment building itself. His steps were light.

"I like to go this way, so I can catch her out if she's forgotten to lock her window," Dom told Kiddo as they ascended. As if, in his enthusiasm, he'd forgotten himself how Kiddo always followed him up these stairs.

Sure enough, the window slid open the moment he tested it.

They heard her wheezing away to herself inside.

"Miss Dorris?" Dom called. "Can we come in?"

The wheezing paused, before there was a cough.

There was a slow shuffle of footsteps.

"Is that my Raze?" her thin voice asked breathily, and she appeared at the window with a glad smile. "And he's with his ..."

"Kiddo," Kid reminded her patiently. He drove her home most nights, but she struggled with almost everyone's name.

"I just filled the teapot," she revealed with a warm gleam in her eye, as if it were a cheeky secret.

Kiddo and Dom climbed inside her apartment, locking the window behind them, and Kiddo made the tea.

"I think this cup will suit you," Miss Dorris told Kiddo, selecting it from her display cabinet. "While Raze would like this one. And here is my favourite of all time."

She'd had a different favourite one last visit, but Kiddo always took the utmost care of every piece of Miss Dorris' fine china anyway – hardly knowing how to deal with things that were so dainty.

Dom herded her to the table and busied himself about her when she was seated. He chose a pair of slip on shoes to swap with her crochet slippers, fastened her favourite peacock brooch to her snuggly jumper, and then smoothed a warm hat over her shock of white hair.

"Beautiful," he announced with approval. "But, Miss Dorris, why is it so cold in here?"

"Beautiful," she replied to him sunnily, cupping his cheek. "But, why are you so gaunt, dear? Are you eating?"

Dom glanced at the fridge, where a late notice told them that she'd forgotten to keep up with her bills.

She turned her head to give a small cough.

Kiddo set her cup on the table and took the notice papers out from under a spangly butterfly magnet, pocketing them. He would take care of it on the car ride.

He smiled at a slightly faded piece of note paper, with a short letter and a happy face on it that Dom had drawn her a while back. She never moved it from the front and centre of her fridge.

"Our housekeeper Raff is always throwing food at me," Dom assured her. "But maybe he's not as great of a cook as my Kiddo."

"I'll start cooking for you again," Kiddo answered bluntly. "Even if all you want to stomach is greasy balls of fried fat."

"Good brain food," Dom approved. "Just what I need."

"How romantic," Miss Dorris said as she finished her tea dreamily.

Kiddo rarely drank caffeine, so Dom quickly downed both his and Kiddo's teas in single gulps – swigging like a mighty giant drinking from two thimbles.

"I think you're ready to go," Dom decided, pumping a fist against his chest as the liquid went down in a hurry.

"I'm going?" Miss Dorris' face crinkled, her already wavery voice becoming more uncertain.

"To the clinic," Kiddo prompted her memory. He rinsed the delicate cups carefully at the sink.

"You have a cough," Dom told her.

"I do?"

"You do. And we have doctors."

She held his arm as he escorted her out to the elevator and Kiddo locked up.

Dom buckled her into the front seat of her old car. He drove them back to base while Kiddo worked out a recurring payment for her bills on his phone, and sent a couple of messages to warn they were on the way.

Kiddo caught Dom's blue eyes in the rear-view mirror, roaming over Kid in the back seat with a mischievous glint.

The night they'd borrowed this car, Kiddo had been sprawled across the back in hiding. Dom had told him then that it was lucky he was busy driving, or he'd be on that back seat too.

Kiddo smirked and rolled his eyes.

When they got to Hato's base Dom drove all the way into the open garage.

"Is … that … Sparkles?" Miss Dorris wheezed as Sparks took a moment to greet her.

"So good to see Raze's nanna," Sparks told Miss Dorris lovingly. "One of my apprentices will check your car over while you're here."

"Sparkles suits you," Kiddo told Sparks, kissing the top of her head.

He didn't have to try hard to catch up to Dom and Miss Dorris, as they shuffled their way to a door that was a relatively new addition to the ground level of the warehouse.

Frazzle and Doctor Daleeah's medical wing was an extension attached to the original complex. There were connecting corridors so that Frazzle and Daleeah had their own space, but they were also a protected part of the base.

"Such a nice facility," Miss Dorris commented, wide eyed as they stepped into a spacious, bright waiting room. "I'm not sure I can afford this clinic."

"Hush," Dom tutted. "You don't have to worry about things like that here."

Daleeah came to meet them. She'd been in the larger ward for recovery and long stays. Beyond that, there were testing and pathology rooms, a small private surgery, and even an equipped radiology room.

"Welcome Miss Dorris, I am Dalee," Daleeah greeted the elderly lady, at once captivating Miss Dorris with her natural charm. "I will be your doctor today. Your grandson can help you into my office."

The doctor was working, so her coat and trousers were basic. But nothing else about Daleeah was ever plain. Her hijab was a sky blue, she radiated calm elegance, and Miss Dorris was totally reassured by her.

Dom escorted Miss Dorris into Daleeah's private consultation room, and Kiddo leaned against the reception desk to wait.

He was expecting company, as apart from paying Miss Dorris' bills online, the texts he'd also sent on the car ride had been to two specific people.

"Kid." Hato made the large waiting room seem suddenly smaller as he stepped out of Frazzle's office, with Frazzle close behind.

"Hey Hato. Fraz," Kiddo greeted them both quietly.

"Is all well Kiddo?" Frazzle's English was much more confident under Daleeah's influence. "You are taking good care?"

Kiddo directed a pointed look at Hato. "I'm on top of my medication. But I wasn't texting to bring you here for me. I actually wanted a word with you about Dom, before he comes out."

"Yes? You are worried?" Frazzle asked, though he didn't seem surprised.

Hato rubbed his jaw. "Dominic is ... less energetic than normal."

Kiddo nodded. "He is performing as well as ever for his recruits and in front of the other gangs. But off duty, he isn't himself. And he hardly does seem to be off duty – doing extra patrols of his own all the time."

"He may be struggling, not to have any power ..." Frazzle thought the sentence through. "Over the Yorak situation. Waiting is, stressful."

"He has a low appetite – even though Raff is determinedly

feeding him. He often has headaches, tiredness, and can become vague," Kiddo listed. "I get that it could definitely be mental and emotional strain. But can we also check that it isn't anything else, just in case?"

Frazzle glanced up as Dom closed the door to Daleeah's office to wait for Miss Dorris outside.

"Hey guys," he said.

"Dominic," Hato rumbled.

"You are too skinny," Frazzle asserted. "Come for a blood test."

Dom was startled. "Huh?"

Frazzle beckoned Dom to follow, and left the room.

Dom blinked at Kiddo.

Kiddo shrugged. "What's the harm?"

Dom blinked at Hato.

"Hurry," Hato warned. "The new clinic is big. Don't want to get lost."

| 6 |

Six

Sparks' apprentices had given Miss Dorris' vehicle a fast clean as well as a speedy once over, and Miss Dorris had told Dom how proud she was of him for getting a blood test.

Miss Dorris had then sung them church songs on the car trip back to her apartment, and had watched as they'd stuck post-it notes around her place to remind her to take her medication as soon as she woke up each morning.

"Thank you for that," Dom nudged Kiddo with his shoulder as they ambled away from her building. "It made my heart full."

"The blood test?" Kiddo jibed. "Surely that does the opposite."

"Hmmf, yes," Dom laughed dryly. "Losing blood was a different twist for average date day event number four."

"Average days include health checks and errands," Kiddo defended. "As well as lazy, late lunches." He led the way across the road to a café.

Kiddo chose some sandwiches for them while Dom minded their outdoor table.

"Don't look now," Dom remarked casually when he was opening the sandwich packaging. "But there is a hungry child watching us from behind some cars. She has a mean, street vibe. Angry fists in her pockets and a scowl on her face."

Kiddo refrained from looking. "Do we know her? A local?"

"Mmm. I've seen her around the area a few times before," Dom mused. "But she never actually *meant* for me to see her. Wonder what's different today."

"How old?"

Dom chewed thoughtfully on a mouthful of bread, egg and lettuce.

"Maybe eight," he speculated after a few moments. "Scrawny. Red hair. A mess."

Kiddo's shoulders dipped. "She sounds like my baby snatcher from yesterday."

Dom poured them both glasses of water from the tall, chilled bottle on the table. Then he pushed his glass and the other half of his sandwich in the packet toward a spare chair at their table.

He made a 'take a seat' motion with his hand, gazing directly over Kiddo's shoulder so that the child couldn't mistake the fact that he'd seen her.

Kiddo calmly sipped at his own water, trusting that Dom would stop the child from murderously lunging at his back if she got the guts up to approach.

Dom watched, straight faced and unmoving, as the child apparently did decide to muster the courage to come out into the open.

Kiddo felt the back of his neck prickle as she took steps towards their table.

"Hey baby snatcher," Dom greeted her – not unkindly. "Here to catch or kill us?"

There was a tough little scoffing sound. She was close enough now that Kiddo could turn his head to see her easily.

"Here to watch you." Her voice had such bravado. "But so far the show's been boring."

"It has been a luxuriously normal day," Dom agreed pleasantly.

"What changed since yesterday?" Kiddo asked her. "Your group seemed keen enough to do more than watch then?"

She crossed her arms. She was all freckles and glares.

Her eyes darted to the sandwich and then away again, but Kiddo and Dom had noticed.

"That group's Hunter got too greedy," she glowered. "Trying to get you for himself without putting in any effort," she flicked her eyes at Kiddo. "That's not the plan."

Dom leaned his chin on both hands. "What's the plan?" he asked nicely.

She snorted. Then she darted forward and swiped the sandwich, before disappearing fast.

"Wow," Kiddo stared at where she'd stood.

"Wow," Dom sighed. "That is not a great situation."

Kiddo tapped his fingers on the table. "She definitely could be one of the most terrifying snatchers we've ever come across," he conceded.

The idea of one so young and so malleable being torturously conditioned, and already being so experienced in the snatcher life ...

"However," Kiddo tried for a lighter tone. "Dwelling on that isn't part of our average date day." He pushed the other half of his own sandwich across the table.

"What's next?" Dom queried, and obediently resumed eating.

"A leisurely stroll back to base."

"Ahuh."

"A quick stop off first, though."

"Oh?"

"Well actually, we're going to pick up fish and chips for an early dinner."

Dom closed the sandwich package. "I just finished late lunch."

"True," Kiddo assented. "But Pash and Sparks are going to be starving, and we haven't really had heaps to eat today."

"You will have had your quota for oil," Dom grinned. "But that's very nice of us to feed Sparks and Pash too."

"Raff was rather put out when I told him how many of us wouldn't be needing dinner."

Dom smirked. "He really does love offering me every morsel he can. I'm his personal project."

When Kiddo led Dom up to the base's rooftop garden, Sparks and Pash had already set out some picnic rugs, and the group spread the paper parcel out between them.

"Deep fried, golden goodness," Pash cooed over the food lovingly.

He was rocking a closely shaven head and stubbled chin tonight. With extra thick, gold coloured eyeliner.

"For a model and influencer, your diet habits are shocking," Kiddo remarked, while ripping a 'plate' of paper for Dom, and piling him up with deep fried golden goodness too.

"Don't you worry your pretty little head," Pash sighed happily. "Being a beloved model by day, and a Raze or a Lair bouncer by night keeps me super fit."

Sparks cracked a can of soft drink open. "Never mind your contractors. Teddy would tell you if you started to go soft in the middle."

Pash chuckled appreciatively. "That she would. Teddy was the one who told me to stop being so beige during my neutrals phase last season. We settled on taupe." He grinned at the memory. "I think my followers actually love Teddy more than they love me, based on all the attention our selfies together get."

"But Teddy's advice isn't always so good," Dom warned, leaning over to give Kiddo a specially chosen, particularly crunchy chip.

Kiddo smiled and accepted the gift. Dom knew those ones were his favourites.

"It was Teddy's idea for you to raid Velvet's wardrobe," Dom went on.

Pash leaned back on his elbows. "Velvet hasn't been back in ages to find that one out, anyway," he answered a little wistfully. "And it was a good lesson to find out that her dresses are way too tight on me."

"She's going to find out sometime that her favourite purple body suit burst at the seams," Sparks teased. "And who else would have been so silly as to go into Velvet's wardrobe?"

"Teddy said I could use her as a shield," Pash shrugged,

flopping down now to chew and stare up at the late afternoon sky. "Velvet wouldn't hurt Teddy."

Dom sprawled out too, cushioning his head with his arms. "Teddy is about half a body shorter than you, and Velvet's signature death stroke is a fist to the head. So your shield will be safe while your face will not."

They were quiet for a few moments as they reminisced about the very lethal Velvet and the other absent Razes.

"It'll be so good to see them all for Fraz and Dalee's wedding," Sparks commented at last.

"Yeah," Kid agreed hollowly. "It will."

| 7 |

Seven

They stayed spread out on the rugs until the sun set, when both Pash and Kiddo had to get ready for their evening roles.

Dom gazed up questioningly when Kiddo reached a hand down to him.

"Come on," Kiddo said. "Average date day continues with a trip to your partner's work."

Dom peered at Sparks. "Goody."

"Don't look at me," she giggled. "I don't trust you near explosive liquids while I'm busy talking to Trix. I remember how you earned your nickname."

The restaurant was definitely a safer choice.

Dom allowed himself to be pulled up. "Are you going to give me strawberry milkshakes like Pash gets for visiting the diner?"

"Oh no," Kiddo shook his head. "You'll have to pitch in. There won't be special treatment when you're on the average date day."

Dom tapped his chin. "I see, I see. This could make for as much of an eventful night as I would have had on the streets.

I know Beef Cake visits you on the regular, and he and his gang's boss just can't seem to work me out."

Sparks chuckled at the thought of how her old gang would react to visits from Raze.

"Beef Cake's friend, Dolly, often comes by too," Kiddo agreed. "And *she's* worked you out. Says you're pretty."

Dom snorted. "You're going to keep me locked up in the kitchen, aren't you?"

That was exactly what Kiddo was going to do.

They were going to have fun together, with Kiddo teaching Dom all of the classics.

And as Kiddo had hoped, Dom alternated between taking his lessons very seriously, to having a hoot of a time making an absolute mess.

Whenever the wait staff pushed their way through the swinging kitchen doors they were confronted by a tableau of:

Dom learning to use a set of digital scales.

Kiddo peeling and chopping vegetables ten times more efficiently than Dom.

Dom making a sizable snowman out of a bowl piled with mash.

The other cooks laughing at Dom as he demonstrated the correct technique for pot drumming.

Kiddo holding Dom's hand and furiously searching for the fake 'burn' he had never acquired.

Kiddo holding Dom's hand for the sake of it.

Kiddo rearranging Dom's efforts to pack one of the dishwashers.

Dom sipping a strawberry milkshake and sitting on a benchtop, watching Kiddo do the real cooking.

"Yes, good, that's how it's done," Dom was complimenting Kiddo's julienning for a batch of coleslaw when the door opened next. "That carrot really couldn't have been reduced to ribbons any more finely than that."

"What was this method called again, master?" Kiddo smirked at Dom beside him.

"Julie Anne," Dom replied confidently. And he planted a fast, strawberry kiss on Kiddo's lips. "Julie Anne loves ribbons. I'll remember that."

"Uh, Kid," one of the waiters was hesitant to interrupt.

"What's up?" Kiddo asked. Clearly having a great time.

The waiter sighed. "The man who visited you last night is back."

Kiddo's expression changed from carefree, to incredulous, to irritated.

"Sorry Kid," the waiter sighed. "I could tell he wasn't your favourite person."

"*What?*" Dom tutted. "A mystery man is visiting my boyfriend? That is unacceptable."

"This guy's a stiff," the waiter whispered back reassuringly. "He doesn't hold a torch to you, Raze."

"Not even a match," Kiddo patted Dom on the knee. "It'll be Narkon."

Kiddo took up a bowl and ladled a generous helping of that night's special into it – a particularly hearty soup. He set it on a plate with a fresh dinner roll and a spoon on the side.

"Would you watch over the kitchen so it doesn't fall into disarray, great master?" Kiddo asked Dom.

Dom nodded gravely, while vacuuming up strawberry foam with his straw.

"And would you watch over Raze so that the kitchen *really* doesn't fall into disarray?" Kiddo uttered out of the side of his mouth to one of the chuckling cooks.

Kiddo backed out of the swinging doors to turn and place the special in front of Narkon, who was again seated on the same stool from the night before.

"Please enjoy," Kiddo told the chef, his voice flattening almost immediately.

"It sounds like there's a great deal of enjoyment that goes on in the kitchen you run," Narkon commented.

Kiddo took it for more taciturn criticism.

"Mm."

Narkon took a small, contemplative sip of the soup.

"Not going to ask me why I'm back?"

Kiddo's expression was just as flat as his voice had been. "I would hate to pry. So I'll just assume it's the food."

Kiddo made to turn away.

"Actually," Narkon stopped him. "The food is of course enjoyable. But ..."

There was always a 'but' with this man.

"But my business model is more ethical than economical?" Kiddo cut in. "Or my talents are being wasted on the wrong people? Or I'm lazy? Or you're here to save me from my flaws?"

Kiddo rolled his eyes.

Narkon swallowed another mouthful of the soup. He picked at the freshly baked dinner roll.

The chef was about to reply when a waitress approached Kiddo. Yet instead of facing Kid, she stood beside him and addressed Narkon.

She seemed especially timid, and she couldn't meet Narkon's gaze as she nervously fixed her apron, but she was apparently determined to speak.

"I ... know who you are," she told Narkon. "And after what I heard you saying last night ... I can tell what you think Kiddo should really be doing." She cleared her throat.

"It's alright," Kiddo began uncomfortably, but the waitress shook her head.

She took a deep breath. "Kiddo helped me when I was just a customer here," she said shakily. "When my restraining order wasn't working, he *noticed* me. He and the Raze gang looked into what was happening, and stopped it. Then Kiddo hired me. He saved my life," she stammered. "All of the servers and many of the customers are here for a reason. This is more than just a diner."

Her eyes darted up to Narkon, to check that he was patiently listening. Then darted back to the counter.

Kiddo patted her awkwardly on the arm.

"Would you check on Miss Dorris for me?" Kiddo asked her. His face had reddened. "She's already been out today, so I'm surprised she's here tonight."

The waitress relaxed a little, her posture losing its tension. "I spoke to her when she came in," the young woman answered hurriedly. "She said Sundays aren't her only outing days anymore."

Narkon noticed the elderly lady with the afro of white hair and the warm, sloppy jumper. Her teacup was again different to everyone else's, though it was being ignored while she snoozed.

"She also said she would be asleep in her armchair if she were at home alone, so why not nap in company?" the waitress gave a wisp of a smile. "I can drop her at home when my shift ends."

"I'll get one of the recruits to take her car back to her tomorrow," Kiddo was replying gratefully, when he suddenly stiffened.

Narkon and the waitress followed his line of sight, past where he had been gazing at Miss Dorris.

Beyond the nodding elderly lady, peering in through the window, was a little girl with a hard face.

She had to be homeless.

Her fiery curls were a fluffy mess on her head. She was dirty. Undernourished. As if she might have fought for every meal she'd ever had.

Her watchful eyes were on Kiddo.

And she hadn't seen the shadowy group of masked figures sneaking up behind her.

The imperturbable Narkon himself was shaken to notice them, as they'd blended so well into the night.

It was only as they slinked into the light spilling from the diner that they were clear, like sudden apparitions.

Horrifying apparitions at that. Their balaclavas had the

image of giant, bleeding fangs that stretched across where mouths should be.

One of the figures seized the child by the neck, and she was rapidly yanked from view.

It had been so fast, Narkon could hardly believe what he'd witnessed.

Kiddo cursed.

"Don't tell Raze," he told the waitress over his shoulder, already on the move and out the door.

Nobody else seemed to have noticed what had happened beyond the window.

| 8 |

Eight

There were six of them. Masked up with freakish fang mouths, and circling the baby snatcher as if she wasn't one of their own.

But snatchers were like that. No close bonds or loyalties to anything other than their work and their own survival.

They'd been quick about hauling the child away from streetlights and crowds, and it had even taken Kiddo a minute to quietly find them in a clearing off the road, a distance from Kid's Place.

The clue to follow had been the intermittent sound of the baby snatcher clawing and cussing up a storm while one of them held her by the hair.

"You haven't even graduated to the mask yet," one of the snatchers growled at the baby snatcher. "So what makes you so special? Why'd he choose you?"

The shadowy outline of the baby snatcher hissed and kicked, not caring that her hair might get pulled out by the roots.

Another snatcher slapped her face.

"Nothing! No reason!" she blurted. "It's cos I'm small and my whole team got wiped out anyway!"

Wiped out by Kiddo.

Kiddo tried to remember this could all be a trap. The exact same trap he'd fallen for yesterday, with even the same bait. He continued to creep forward carefully.

"Oh, come on. As if even your Hunter is dead. Shouldn't *they* get the honour of this mission?"

The snatchers shook her by her hair so that she cried out.

"I've been working separate for ages! But the Hunter truly is dead too, so I was going to be reassigned anyway!"

"Pft. You probably killed your team yourself. You'd like the glory of getting Yorak's favourite Razes for him yourself."

"No!" she wailed.

"No? Well I bet it's what you're planning to do on your little private mission now," a snatcher laughed.

"*We're* young and sweet," one of the others sulked. "It's not fair that she got the job."

"You've all had your growth spurts," the baby snatcher whimpered. "It's not my fault!"

"Ah well. They won't have a choice but to pick one of us once you're gone," a lanky silhouette chortled. Then he balled up his fist and slammed it into the baby snatcher's middle so that her legs curled up.

Snatchers pressed in on either side of her, taking hold of her small throat and her little arms and legs.

Kiddo forgot about this potentially being another trap. He forgot about the baby snatcher specifically being out to help Yorak against the Raze gang.

All he saw was a child who was about to be literally torn limb from limb.

Kiddo sprinted forward and ripped two snatchers off the girl by their collars.

Startled, the group turned to face this new threat, dropping the child and almost trampling her.

Kiddo ducked beneath swinging arms, grabbed for the girl's ankle, and slid her out from the fray.

He sent her skidding across the grass, even as he felt purposeful fists start to rain down over the back of his head and shoulders.

He grunted, standing up fast despite the weight of their assault. He grabbed one flying wrist, and jerked that snatcher's body forward into his own fist.

The snatcher's head jerked back – the rest of the body following suit to topple to the ground.

Then Kid felt the weight of another snatcher landing on his back – a pair of arms squeezing tight around his neck.

Kiddo angrily elbowed backward, jabbing the attacker in the ribs, but then he felt the snatcher's arms become limp and then the weight disappeared from Kid's shoulders.

The cavalry had arrived.

Kiddo hated to think that Dom's easy evening had been ruined, though Kid was glad to have the help.

Kiddo seized the shirtfront of another snatcher and drove his knuckles into every fleshy bit of body he could reach.

Nobody else went for Kiddo's back, and there were the sounds of a fight behind him. However, it wasn't until Kiddo heard the shrill voice of the baby snatcher, shouting at the other snatchers, that the fight truly eased.

"He's one of Yorak's favourite Razes!" the girl cried out. "You hurt him for real and you're dead!"

The snatchers wheeled about in the darkness – staggering, bruised, but clearly still dominating in numbers and strength.

It would be impossible to tell who they were fighting in such poor light, yet they heeded the girl's words – pulling back.

Squinting and panting, Kiddo was surprised that the baby snatcher was still huddling where she'd rolled to a stop. He could just make out her shadowy form, hugging her knees.

Why hadn't she run away?

There were curses, and Kiddo was shoved backward by two snatchers who came to swipe their floppy comrade from Kiddo's grips.

But after they had collected their more battered fellows, they did retreat fast into the darkness.

Panting, Kiddo couldn't help but to hurry to the baby snatcher.

He saw that her face was wet with tears, and she wiped roughly at her nose – her expression pitiful.

She knew they had truly meant to kill her. A group of gangly teenage snatchers who hated that she was skating by on being cute.

His heart thudded with an odd relief that they hadn't succeeded, and Kiddo surprised both of them, kneeling down and putting an arm around the child's shoulders.

She froze. As if she didn't know what to do with a hug.

And he cringed – not having meant to intimidate her.

He didn't pull her in or move again. But for a moment *she*

scrambled in and let her small face burrow against his chest. She nestled her forehead against his t-shirt and sniffled.

"It's alright. You're safe now," Kiddo's saviour spoke to her out of the shadows then.

This time it was both Kiddo and the girl who stiffened.

The girl, because she realised exactly what she was doing. Kiddo, because he realised that that was not Dom's voice.

Narkon?

Kiddo collected himself quickly. He gave the girl's shoulders a squeeze.

"Come in for a meal?" he asked her gently.

"Piss off!" she half sobbed and half spat, trying to get her bravado back up.

She threw off his arm and booted him in the chest so that he fell back on his haunches.

She checked that she hadn't lost anything from her pockets, as if he might've just got close so he could rob her.

Then she scrambled up and ran as hard as she could in the opposite direction to the snatchers.

Kiddo sighed.

For the second day in a row he dusted her footprint from his clothing.

"Are you alright?" Narkon asked. He stooped to pull Kiddo up by his arm.

Kiddo accepted the help, while regarding Narkon warily.

"You're the last person I thought I'd find beating up snatchers," Kiddo commented. "Ruffians don't last long in the upmarket kitchen environment."

Narkon released Kiddo's arm and followed him back to the diner.

"I saw a child getting abused by a group of bullies, and only one person out there trying to save her," Narkon answered. "Of course I was going to lend a hand."

Kiddo snorted. "*Bullies.* You can hardly call a snatcher a bully."

He tugged Narkon to a stop on the perimeter of the diner's lights.

"Neaten yourself up a bit," he instructed. He rubbed at his sternum. The footprint was gone, but it did still smart.

The two of them straightened themselves out. Thankfully they hadn't really been marked – just dishevelled.

"What is a snatcher?" Narkon asked suspiciously. "And why would they want to harm a child?"

Kiddo opened the diner's tinkling door, and gestured for Narkon to enter. "It's in their job description."

Narkon frowned in disbelief. He sat back heavily on his stool.

"Who was the Yorak character they mentioned? And … wasn't Raze your partner?"

"Look, don't worry about it," Kiddo told the chef firmly.

"Don't worry about what?" Dom burst out of the kitchen, his arms lined with plates of food, and the image of gaily laughing cooks showing briefly through the swinging doors behind him.

Narkon opened his mouth, full of questions, but Kiddo elbowed him in the ribs so that he closed it.

"*You* are not worrying about anything today," Kiddo replied.

"Course I'm not," Dom agreed. He expertly delivered plate after plate to each booth, as if he'd been born to the role.

Admiring gazes followed him around the diner, as well as awe-struck whispers of the word '*Raze*'.

Since the gang had decided to become an open challenger to the snatcher world, the original Raze had also become a widely known figure in this area. The ambiguous stories that had surrounded him since he had first become Raze years ago had circulated and grown now.

Law enforcers, gangsters, and people of the streets had known for a long time about the snatchers too, and they mostly knew the real importance of the Raze gang. But the fascination and oddly enthusiastic fear revolving around the original Raze himself had even spread to normal members of their community. Those who simply thought of him as a vigilante in general.

Rumours of legendary proportions did half of Dom's work for him, and he and his recruits could put their focus where it was most needed.

"Who's this?" Dom asked sweetly when he was done, eye-balling Narkon and slinging a possessive arm around Kiddo's shoulders. He knew perfectly well who it was.

Narkon eyed the endless tattoos covering Dom's visible skin, and the whispers that he'd stirred up like a breeze around the room. Whispers of trepidation as well as appreciation.

Narkon was trying to decide if Kiddo really was in with

the wrong crowd. Or if maybe the 'wrong' crowd wasn't actually the *worst* crowd out there.

"This is Chef Narkon," Kiddo told Dom.

"And you must be –" Narkon began.

"RAAAZEEE!"

Dom cocked an eyebrow.

"Beef Cake," he greeted the young thug over his shoulder.

"Oh my God, Raze," Beef Cake gushed. "If you're here, why'd I get a bunch of messages from the Bullets to say they were in an uproar? Your recruits are going through our base as we speak!"

"Sounds like Quicklips is doing a good job leading the crew tonight," Kiddo answered.

"And if there's such a buzz over our visits, it also sounds like you guys still have some juicy things to hide," Dom drawled. "I'll make sure we're even more thorough next time."

Beef Cake back peddled; hands up. "You're welcome any time man," he promised. "I'm sure the others will be jealous I bumped into you. 'Specially Dolly."

Kiddo snickered. "Sit down Beef Cake, the servers know you're after a coffee."

Beef Cake gladly retreated to a booth, where he, ironically, was amenably welcomed by a bunch of older rival thugs from the Dire gang.

They appeared to be commiserating over Beef Cake's run in with Raze.

"Did you hear about that neck thing he does?" one of the Dires shivered.

Dom had already moved on. "I should get Miss Dorris home," he said to Kiddo. "I'll take her car and walk back."

Kiddo had done the exact same thing countless times. Including last night. And Dom had every ability to protect himself on the streets. Yet Kiddo somehow didn't like the idea of letting him go off alone right now – while he wasn't entirely himself.

"No need, I'm finishing up soon," the timid waitress from earlier told Dom shyly. She was filling a mug of coffee for Beef Cake. "Kiddo and I already worked it out," she gave Dom a wavery smile.

"Well, thank you," Dom gave her a charming smile of his own in return.

"It's for the best," Kiddo nodded seriously. "Your skills are still required in the kitchen."

"Hmm," Dom thoughtfully withdrew his arm from Kiddo. "I haven't heard anything clattering from in there for a while. They must be slacking off."

Dom circled the counter and re-entered the kitchen to a round of cheers from the jovial staff.

Narkon shook his head. "I *really* want to know what the story is here."

"If you haven't grown up knowing the snatcher story, then it's better for you not to find that one out," Kiddo negated.

This man certainly did not seem the type to stomach such unpalatable, hard truths.

"Seems like there's a story to the Raze gang and this diner too," Narkon commented. "And if the snatcher story is such an awful one, surely spreading the word isn't a bad thing?"

"As I said," Kiddo folded his arms. "Don't worry about it. You're just passing through on your contract, and then you'll be back in your own world. You'll be safer there."

"I don't have to rush straight into retirement when the contract is up," Narkon mused. "And my nights and weekends are free. Perhaps I could be of service to you."

"No need." Kiddo reached over to slide Narkon's half full bowl away. "Your soup's gone cold."

Narkon openly chuckled at the obvious hint this time. He took out his wallet, but Kiddo waved him away, despite the 'pay if you can' rule.

"Are you going to ask me to come again?" Narkon asked.

"No," Kiddo answered. "But I'll thank you for your help earlier. And wish you a good rest of your night."

| 9 |

Nine

"Hungry?" Raff asked them when they got home.

"Kiddo's been sating my appetites all day," Dom answered nefariously.

"I'm good, thanks," Kiddo coughed. "Have a nice night."

Raff nodded at them as they passed through the kitchen. He watched as Dom practically bounced up the stairway toward the bedroom level of the base.

Unlike most nights since not long after Raff's arrival, Dom was light footed and at ease. Returning a little to his usual self.

"You missed the bedroom," Kiddo whispered, though he calmly followed Dom further upwards.

"Oh no. Did I?" Dom whispered back.

He slipped into the library, where they'd started their day.

Now it was all shadows and silver beams; the moon huge beyond the wide, arched window.

Kiddo caught up in time to see Dom leaning innocently against a wall panel that was identical to all the others.

But with a slight backward push on his particular section,

Dom was slipping into a hidden room, his blue eyes daring Kiddo to follow.

Kid grinned, doing just that.

It was almost pitch black in the narrow space, but Kiddo didn't feel for the light switch, and he didn't mind when the panel slowly swung back into place.

"Why aren't you panicking?" Dom breathed from right behind Kiddo.

"Didn't you and Start design these hidey-holes as safe rooms?" Kiddo queried. "Not panic rooms?"

Dom had once needed an intricate knowledge of the 'behind the scenes', unused spaces of the warehouse. Back when he'd been spying on the gang.

Start had been only too happy to roll out the floor plan of the warehouse when Dom had suggested they make use of those spaces while the other extensions and upgrades were happening.

Kiddo felt Dom trace a hand over his shoulder blades and then down his spine.

"So you feel safe?" Dom asked.

His arm snaked around Kiddo's waist now.

"With you? Always."

Dom stepped closer, and pressed his lips to the back of Kiddo's neck.

"It's like you tell me each night when you mumble in your dreams," Kiddo went on, softening at the memory. "You say: 'I'm safe with you. You love me. You are always helping me'."

"Huh," Dom's voice was surprised. "Must be super tired to talk in my sleep."

Dom's confident fingers traced their way over the skin just above Kiddo's waistline.

"Never too tired to sweet talk, it seems," Kiddo joked.

"To sweet talk you, at any rate," Dom affirmed. "One full day with you, eating greasy food, catching up with good people, and cracking jokes in the kitchen ... it's the best I've felt in ages," Dom confessed contentedly. "I was so drained."

Kiddo turned slowly in Dom's hold. "You needed to recharge."

"Oh and I did," Dom leaned forward to purr against Kiddo's ear. There was a mischievous note to his voice.

"You're not done yet," Kiddo warned. "The holiday continues tomorrow."

It was a narrow space, the size of a walk-in wardrobe. And when Dom suddenly drove Kiddo backward, it was only moments before his shoulder blades were pressed up against the wall.

"Another supposedly mediocre day tomorrow?" Dom queried.

He pressed his lips to the side of Kiddo's throat, probably feeling how fast Kid's pulse was racing.

"Not fast food ... and no average pass times tomorrow," Kiddo answered as he got his breath back. "I'll wine and dine you properly for our next date day."

"Ohhh?" Dom ran a hand up, under Kiddo's tee, leaving a trail of prickling goosebumps. "I'll make sure to wear something nice," he promised.

On the topic of clothing, Kiddo found himself being stripped of his shirt.

He groaned despite himself as Dom's kisses and hands

travelled over his skin. The stinging marks over his chest and stomach from earlier became pleasure points that overrode any pain.

"You are so good at throwing me up against walls," Kiddo managed.

"Uh-huh," Dom granted. "You're not so bad at it yourself."

Japan.

In Miss Lotus' tunnels.

When they had made their relationship official.

Kiddo felt his jeans button loosen with a deft tug from invisible fingers.

"The walls of these hidden rooms aren't very thick, are they?" Kiddo gasped.

There went the zipper.

Then there was pressure from that unseen hand.

"Nope."

When he felt Dom's grip settle around his hips like handles, Kiddo bit his knuckles.

Shit.

Keep it together.

Shit.

Keep it quiet.

Shit.

Ohhhhhhh.

| 10 |

Ten

"She's followed us again," Kiddo remarked.

"Yup," Dom swung Kiddo's hand, unconcerned.

He'd worn his most presentable black jeans and a pressed button-up shirt as promised.

Dom of course also carried the scent of Kiddo's own cologne with him too.

"If she wants half my sandwich this time, it'll cost her," Dom remarked.

He watched as a doorman opened the door to the fine restaurant Kiddo had picked for them.

"We're not here for the sandwiches," Kiddo replied. "We're here to taste the tiniest morsels of decoratively arranged delicacies, so that we can say we definitely prefer diner food. And for the sake of enjoying a different kind of date."

Dom tapped on the glass of an expansive fish tank as they stopped to wait in the entryway.

"Let's not order the seafood, now that I've gazed into its eyes," Dom suggested – sharing a meaningful look with a giant lobster. "He's just a humungous, pinchy version of Duncan Jr."

They were led to a table by a window overlooking the street, where they could see the red head of the baby snatcher in the distance. She was wandering back and forth, probably scuffing a pebble up and down the pavement out of boredom.

"Oh my lord, yessssss," Dom sank down into the plush dining chair as if he'd never felt such luxury. Then he caught Kiddo's laugh. "I mean ... oh my lord ... it's a bit much isn't it? Who needs their butt to feel so extravagant during a meal?"

"Give me a blanket on the rooftop any day," Kiddo teased.

"Oh my loooooooord," Dom breathed as he ran a lotus tattooed finger over the fine linen tablecloth. "Let's not order tomato soup either. There'll be a special place in hell for anyone who splats on this."

"We'll have to bring Sparks here," Kiddo decided. "She'll get a kick out of it."

He had booked for her just in case, but the third chair at their table was empty. The garage had been too swamped for her to get out.

Dom opened the leather bound menu in front of him.

"Lordylordylordylordy," he whistled faintly as he read one unfamiliar dish after another. "The prices haven't been listed."

There were other diners spread out around the restaurant, though their conversations were low and didn't carry over the soft music floating through the dining area.

Each table felt like an intimate space. The sounds of cutlery lightly making contact on expensive plates, and of fine glassware being lifted and clinked, were the loudest noises in the space.

"They don't want you to die of shock *before* you've eaten yourself into debt," Kiddo surmised in a confidentially lowered voice.

"I can't see any Julie Annes, or tater mash monsters," Dom leaned forward, speaking just as secretively.

"That was a snowman in a bowl," Kiddo corrected in an intent whisper, tilting closer too. "Nothing monstrous about it."

"Sure, but 'mash monster' rolls off the tongue," Dom answered. He peered around as if someone might be trying to eavesdrop, and spoke covertly. "That's just a tip, if you're going to put it on your specials board."

"Any dim-sims or deep fried golden goodness on the menu?" Kiddo enquired in almost a murmur.

"No. Nothing I recognise to be edible," Dom conceded furtively. "You best order."

They both straightened purposefully as their drinks arrived, and Kiddo confidently picked a few surprise dishes for them to share.

"Ohhhhhhhhhhhhhhh –"

"Lord?" Kiddo finished for Dom, who had just sipped at his red wine.

"I bet even your chilled water tastes a million dollars," Dom chuckled. "This is the best."

Kiddo tested his water. "Mmm. Can definitely taste the expense."

"You would hate working in a place like this for a day job," Dom surmised. "Too stuffy."

"It's nice for a special date. It would be a nightmare for a lifetime," Kiddo agreed. "I love how Kid's Place has character. And it's become part of our gang's community watch."

"Yes ... definitely don't let Narkon sway you into this lifestyle ..." Dom warned absently. He closed his eyes to breathe in the aroma of a passing dish. "A nightmare. Totally against our principles."

"Actually Narkon did a complete backflip last night," Kiddo admitted. "Rather than forcing me out of the diner game, he suddenly offered to get in on it."

"Really?" Dom blinked. "Wow. What did you say?"

"I said no," Kiddo answered. "Politely."

"His name and influence could be helpful," Dom reflected. "As well as his skill set. If he really was up for helping out."

Kiddo tried to picture it. This was the kitchen shark, who was used to crowds bowing down in adulation, or even cowering down with intimidation. Paying top dollar to taste his skills night after night.

Dom's eyes lit up as their own skilfully presented plates were placed between them.

The one in front of Dom featured an aesthetic dash of puréed peas and three almost bite-sized pieces of beef.

In front of Kiddo there was a plate with three pieces of perfect spinach and ricotta filled ravioli, drizzled in a cream sauce.

The centre dish held three stuffed mushrooms, filled with a tender white meat, and topped with golden crumbs.

"Kiddo ... they put a tiny twig with leaves on my meat

cube," Dom whispered in fascination, poking at the sprig of rosemary garnish with his fork. "This place is crazy."

"I don't think this is the kind of place that will give us a takeout container for Sparks' share." Kiddo started distributing one of each of the foods onto Dom's plate and then his own.

"We could put the third helping into a napkin and sneak it to the baby snatcher," Dom suggested. "I know she's out to ruin us, but she's skin and bones."

Dom had hardly bounced back to normal himself after only one day of Kiddo force feeding him. But the child outside truly was just a fierce little skeleton.

Kiddo couldn't help but pull his phone out to catch a candid photo. Dom's mesmerised glee was irresistible as he hardly had to touch his beef piece before it collapsed into tender strips for the eating.

"I do have to warn you," Kiddo said, still smiling as he settled his phone back on his lap. "The mushroom is a betrayal of the new friendship you made earlier."

Dom appeared to be having some kind of spiritual moment with the beef.

"It's my crustacean buddy, isn't it?" he asked emotionally.

Kiddo nodded.

Dom considered it.

"We hardly knew each other," he decided. And sampled the mushroom next.

Kiddo couldn't deny the almost miraculous quality of such pricey dishes, and despite the sparse arrangement of the food on each plate, one serve of each type did leave them pleasantly satisfied.

Kid lounged back contentedly when he was done. He felt his phone vibrate in his lap, showing an alert from Flip's team.

Opening the group chat, he read that there had been only minor injuries all round after a scouting mission in Egypt. But he decided not to say anything that might shift Dom's focus back to work yet.

"Do you remember in Tokyo when I thought you would starve?" Dom reminisced; sneakily pushing the third serve of each plate onto a napkin. "Your chopsticks game was really low."

"Do you remember last night when I got you to peel some potatoes?" Kiddo ruminated airily. "Your peeler game was non-existent."

Dom smirked. "Do you remember last night, in that dark, enclosed space?"

He folded the napkin over to hide the small pile of food.

They would have to bump up the tip to cover the theft of the cloth, stitched so nicely with the restaurant's insignia.

"Do you remember the rooftop … when I first got to meet you both?"

Neither of them had felt a ripple of alarm.

For once, they hadn't been hyper aware of their surroundings – seeing threats behind every stranger's smile.

They had been caught up in their own world.

Until the spare chair at their table was pulled back, and a lithe, smartly dressed Wolf took a seat.

Kiddo noticed at least twelve Hunters being directed to various nearby tables, following normally smooth wait staff who now appeared somewhat flustered.

The Hunters weren't dressed inappropriately, or even behaving thuggishly. It was just their numbers, their general threatening vibe … and their sinisterly sharpened fang teeth.

Dom didn't miss a beat. "Piss off. You're ruining date day."

He glowered at the Wolf, yet Yorak just seemed strangely charmed.

Yorak regarded Dom keenly. His eyes – one of palest blue, and the other so dark it was almost black – were full of attentiveness.

Kiddo hoped that what he was typing against the screen on his lap said something like 'call me. Don't speak.'

He managed to press send.

Almost immediately, the group chat lit up with an incoming call from Jingle.

Kiddo nudged the answer button at the same time as jostling the tablecloth to more fully cover his legs.

"You must have had to pre-pay an absolute fortune to get so many last minute tables for your friends," Dom scowled. "What a waste."

Yorak inclined his head thoughtfully. "Their tables are paid. But you already had a spare seat reserved for me."

Rather than analysing the menus before them, the Hunters were all either eyeballing Kiddo and Dom, or observing the innocent patrons within their reach. Hands hovered questionably close to jacket pockets, and it was clear that ordinary people faced more risk right now than Kiddo and Dom themselves.

Yorak waved over a server.

"Bring me something decadent," the Wolf told her. "I want my dessert, and to eat it too."

"Yes, sir," she nodded. Her gaze swept the occupants of the table as she collected the empty plates.

It was subtle, but she seemed to have picked up on the stiffness in Kiddo and Dom – the unspoken tension radiating from them.

She left the napkin – kept safe under Dom's protective hand.

"Are you trying to be cute?" Dom questioned with disgust as she withdrew. "*I want my dessert and to eat it too,*" he mocked. "If your cronies are here to abduct us, why waste time on cake?"

"A waste?" Yorak asked. "You look like you could do with dessert yourself." His eyes raked Dom's frame with a hunger of his own, rather than with concern. "I could share mine with you, if you like."

Dom's jaw dropped with indignation as Yorak languidly reached across the table and took up Dom's unfinished glass of wine, sipping from the exact spot that Dom's lips had touched.

"He's just toying with us," Kiddo remarked in a low voice. "He's not here to do anything in public. And he knows there's not much we can do in such a place either."

Yorak nodded calmly, dragging his tongue across his teeth as he relished the strong taste. "Yes. You are my toys. I'm just here to enjoy you."

"Gross," Dom stated flatly.

This man was horrifyingly, coldly beautiful. He could snatch any heart without the snatcher system behind him. But he wanted the hunt, the power, and to win. The main thing he found attractive about Dom and Kiddo was the idea of owning something nobody else could.

"Is this the first chance you've had to impose yourself on us?" Kiddo asked levelly – as if his pulse wasn't thundering. "Or you especially wanted to spoil this lunch?"

A plate with a bite sized slice of visibly dense, rich chocolate cake was placed before the Wolf. Curved flakes of chocolate had been grated over a dash of cream and sprinkled over a decorative swirl of raspberry.

One small mouthful would likely be so heavy as to delightfully fill the consumer at once.

"Ohhh," Yorak sighed thoughtfully. "There was the matter of recovering from your stabbing," he told Kiddo, without a hint of blame or accusation. Rather, a small smile played at the edges of his lips.

"I've also been busy establishing my Hunters as leaders throughout the snatcher world. Your gang would know, the snatchers greatly need stabilising right now, what with so many bases coming under random attack."

Yorak carved a small portion of the cake away with a petite spoon, and generously offered the spoon to Dom first.

"Taste it," he encouraged. "You truly could do with it. You need to watch your weight."

Dom glowered past the spoon, and Yorak shifted it toward Kiddo, who also ignored it.

"No?" Yorak asked. "Neither of you?"

He waited a moment, and then took the first bite himself instead.

The Wolf closed his eyes as he enjoyed the thick texture and the wealth of flavour. He acted as if he was totally comfortable in their company, and as if they posed absolutely no threat.

Dom's nostrils flared with anger. But the Wolf *was* safe, with so many Hunters ready to tear the serene room apart if Kiddo or Dom so much as moved.

Kiddo could feel his phone going mad against his leg, but thankfully nobody who had answered Jingle's call had made any noise. They would be muted and listening, or furiously getting ready to charge over to the restaurant.

"So you've been setting up team leaders and facilitating collaborative groups?" Dom surmised – unimpressed. "Sounds fun. How about seating plans and sticker charts?"

Yorak set the spoon down after a few moments of appreciating that one bite, at last opening his eyes to regard them again.

"A good business needs strong foundations," he answered smoothly. "And then it needs to drum up demand and supply."

Kiddo was getting sick of hearing about good business strategies.

"As you are aware, I've been garnering buyer interest with a few newbie Raze auctions," Yorak went on. "And while those Razes aren't impressive enough to be keepers, their owners do enjoy getting creative, and any footage they circulate of their fun is of course helpful to me."

Dom had paled.

The graduate recruits.

"Even the little attempts and run-ins you've personally faced with different Hunters and their snatcher teams have just been exciting ways to keep exclusive buyers interested while I've been getting ready," Yorak informed them. "We run a betting channel, you know. Counting the odds of how much damage each side will take, and gambling on if we'll really 'catch' you at last."

This time Yorak reached forward to take up Kiddo's glass of water, rinsing his mouth slowly.

"You almost make it *too* easy to run daily bets," he told Dom. "Out with your team or out on your lonesome every chance you get."

He leaned in much closer than necessary to put Kiddo's glass back, breathing deeply, as if trying to memorise Kid's aftershave brand.

"But I'm grateful for those opportunities. We do need to show our buyers that it's hard work, to catch a Raze," he explained.

Kiddo gave in and took the bait. "How exactly does one demonstrate to their buyer audience that it's hard work?"

He noticed a Huntress cracking her knuckles at a nearby table. Her face was flinty.

Yorak's lips curled. "I should show you one time," he mused. "How incredible you were just a day ago, with your precise knife work in that alley." He folded his hands in his lap. "The live stream was quite literally cut when you took down the Hunter. The bodycam was considerably damaged."

Kiddo's skin crawled as he absorbed the fact that the Razes were being filmed by the people they fought.

"You don't seem upset by your losses."

He tried not to grit his teeth as he was grinding the words out.

"No," Yorak agreed. "Anyone you've killed paid the price for failure. And on the other hand, every dramatic base collapse or small-scale battle caught on film has tripled your gang's worth. Having so many killed in 'the hunt' for you makes you all the more precious. In fact, every scratch on you is a mark of survival, and every death you rack up adds another zero to the price tag."

Yorak surprised Kiddo, briefly reaching up to trace the bruise along Kid's jaw.

Dom's knee hit the table as, for a moment, he couldn't contain his outrage.

"Would you stop flirting with us?!" Dom hissed dangerously.

It was lucky he hadn't squashed the napkin of food in his fist.

Yorak settled back in his chair. "But there's only so far I can go with driving up prices. So now I'm ready for the next phase."

"Great," Dom growled. "Phase off then. Get a new hobby."

"Oh no," Yorak chuckled. "Watching you has made me want you more than ever. You remain my personal hobby. I'm always thinking about you."

This man truly had the power to take someone's breath away.

"Obsessed." Dom scoffed.

"Enough small dens have sprung up in this area again, where the action and attraction truly is. Where the heart of the Raze gang dwell. So it is time I stop just visiting to check in on you. I'm ready to stay here, and be here for you properly."

"Don't bother," Kiddo stated. "We don't want you."

Yorak raised his eyebrows. "Weren't you at least thinking of and talking about me, just before? Plotting away so furtively ... so closely ... before you put in your order?"

Even in their current situation, Dom swapped glances with Kid and managed to give the ghost of a smile.

Their comments on mash monsters and dim sims?

"Sure," Kid shrugged. "We have our own plans."

"But *we* don't kiss and tell," Dom said pointedly. "Putting on a big show and being all conversational isn't our style. It's like playing with your food."

Yorak leaned in, breathing deeply again, as if he was pleasantly refreshed by them. Drinking them in like clear mountain air.

"Exactly. You understand me, and I'm coming to understand you. But," he shook his head lightly, like a patient parent correcting a child's mistake. "Talking to you, and 'putting on a show' for you, truly makes my day. I don't want to ever stop playing with you."

This time Yorak surprised Dom, touching an affectionate hand to the side of Dom's head.

Dom flinched, as if the touch had pained him, and smacked the hand away.

The Hunters stirred around them, but Yorak laughed with a light exhaled breath. "My long game isn't just to catch either of you, but to make you both *want* to stay with me. To really have you, my two top Razes, for my own. It'll be symbolic of my own standing in the underworld, and it will be a joyful reward."

Kiddo was ready to gag.

"Right, well we'll see how that pans out," Dom snorted in disbelief.

Yorak nodded. "We will."

After a moment, he gripped the arms of his chair and pushed it back, standing purposefully.

"Thank you for the company," he said politely. "I'd been looking forward to an opportunity like this with such longing."

Then he pushed his chair in, and withdrew.

Without having ordered anything for any of their pre-paid tables, the Hunters all abruptly stood to follow the Wolf out of the room too.

At once the atmosphere became more relaxed again, as if everyone in their area had been unconsciously on edge while The Hunt had been there.

"Your bill, sirs," the waitress placed a slim leather folder on Kiddo and Dom's table – not making eye contact with either of them.

It was unusual etiquette to rush to be rid of guests in such a restaurant.

However Kiddo and Dom took no offense.

They completely understood.

| 11 |

Eleven

Stand down. We're alright. Home soon.

Kiddo didn't read through all of the many messages that had come through during Yorak's visit.

With a quick scan he could see that even the overseas Razes were awake, and repulsed – with Trix and Flip having apparently struck up a competition to describe the Wolf with the foulest expletives they could come up with.

It had become a word for word exchange. An escalating list of singular swears.

More importantly, Jingle's update said that Hato, Quick-lips, Pash, Seethe and the recruits had all now surrounded the restaurant, ready to track and attack if Dom and Kiddo were taken.

"Too late. And it wasn't going to do us much good if we were murdered right here at this table anyway," Dom sighed. "It's such a disadvantage to be the one side in the fight who truly values public safety. The gang could have barged in here and had a right old fight if they'd been quick enough."

"They've taken the recruits to see if they can follow Yorak

and the Hunters," Kid read out the last message. "Or at least to sniff out some of those dens."

He tried not to wonder if this was another manoeuvre of the Wolf's, to draw them into a trap. It was starting to feel like everything was part of Yorak's giant head game.

Kiddo resignedly opened the bill, ready to slip his card inside, when Dom suddenly gripped Kid's wrist – staring at the paper.

"No," Dom uttered in disbelief. "No way."

Kiddo scanned the list until he saw the problem.

Of course.

"That asshole didn't pay his share of the bill," Dom growled. Now truly irate. "*That's* going too far."

"Ugh," Kiddo huffed. He closed the leather wallet and handed it to the waitress. He hardly cared about bumping up tips and stealing napkins right now, though he noticed that Dom must have stowed the food parcel away somewhere.

"So we have to pay for his cake, provide his drinks, and suffer his company," Dom went on, astounded. "What an absolute dic –"

"Thank you so much for dining with us," the waitress hurried back with Kid's card. "We hope you enjoyed your experience."

That was karma for the way Kiddo kept omitting to tell Narkon to please come again.

Dom was still muttering darkly when they passed the fish tank and stepped back out onto the street.

They crossed the road – Dom grumbling all the while.

And the baby snatcher was startled when he stopped right under the tree that she'd thought she'd hidden herself in.

Granted, most people wouldn't have glanced up to notice her peeping face. But wisps of her bright, knotty curls had been out of place amongst the greens.

"You dobbed us in," Dom accused. "Snoop."

Kiddo stared up at her, hands in his pockets.

She would struggle to get away from them if she tried to shimmy down and run, so flight was out, and freeze wasn't her go-to reaction.

She went for fight instead.

"It's my *job*, idiot."

"Your job sucks," Dom informed her sourly.

"You suck."

"No, your *boss* sucks."

Kiddo grimaced. To anyone in the general vicinity, it would appear they were arguing with a tree.

"Yeah, but at least my boss gave me a *cool* job."

"You said we were boring to follow."

"Actually, you're right. So boring."

Kiddo could tell this childish encounter was actually cheering Dom up.

"Then stop following us. Tell Yorak we're dead."

"I'd love to! So die!"

"He wants us alive, though ..."

"Then do that! Whatever!"

"What's your name?"

"Chyeah. 'Sif I'd tell you."

"I could call you Annie, like in the movie."

"Ya think I've seen many movies, idiot?"

She sure made for a much more tragically accurate depiction of a red headed orphan.

"What are you, like eight?"

"What are you? Like, eighty?"

"That's unrealistic," Dom scoffed.

"That's a big word. Where'd you learn it?"

"You're funny," Dom smiled.

"No, YOU'RE..." she paused. "What?"

"And annoying," he added. "But here, catch this."

He slipped his hand into his shirt and withdrew the napkin. Its corners were neatly tied up so that it looked like a vagrant's bundle. Just missing the stick.

He tossed it lightly upward, and she automatically reached out to catch it.

"I honestly hope you won't be the end of us someday," Dom told her.

Then he took Kiddo's hand and they left her to her meal in the tree.

"The snatchers normally sell kids when they're taken that young," Kiddo winced when they got out of earshot. "Especially when they're not the meek kind."

Dom sighed. "Who knows why they wound up keeping her. But maybe she's not completely with them yet. Maybe she hasn't been there too long."

"We have to be careful," Kiddo cautioned them both. "Yorak might want us to get attached."

"A definite possibility," Dom said. "Easier to get attached to that brat than to him," he grumbled.

Dom winced as he pressed his fingertips to the side of his head, where Yorak had laid a hand on him for a moment.

"Bloody touchy-feely creepster. The fiend even got me right on a spot I must keep knocking. He lives to cause pain."

"Imagine if we could save her from him ..." Kiddo mused wistfully. To save her before she was conditioned into a proper snatcher.

He hated to think that things like the alleyway fight, where she'd seen Kiddo himself slice and dice through her group, was something she had grown up seeing. Maybe he especially hated it, because he could recognise himself and so many of their gang members in this child.

"But we're so young to be dads," Dom grinned, dropping his hand from the tender side of his head.

"I dunno, eighty seems plenty old enough to me."

"Ummmm, I might be addled lately. But you've stopped remembering to feed your own fish," Dom retorted.

Kiddo nudged him in the ribs. "That kid wouldn't let either of us forget to feed her. And, I just don't want to over-feed Duncan Jr. I know Raff's already doing it."

Dom was snickering, until they turned the last corner and saw what awaited them.

"Did you just *dawdle* back from a life and death situation?!" Jingle was waiting out the front of the warehouse.

Hey glitter eyeshadow was a sparkling crimson today. It appeared to suit her mood.

"Um..."

They were saved from answering by Sparks dashing out onto the pavement to be caught by them both.

"If I'd just been there ..." she groaned from in amongst their hold.

"He would've had nowhere to sit," Dom chortled. "How awkward."

"Or he would have just watched you eat, spying without us knowing," Jingle snarked, bringing them back to reality. "Cut the jokes. This is serious."

Kiddo pulled Jingle into their group hug too. He was surprised to feel her shaking.

"We are aware," he told her sombrely.

"And we're alright," Dom added, patting her on the back.

Her trembling shoulders sagged.

She didn't say anything.

But it was clear what she was thinking.

For now.

| 12 |

Twelve

"I think I should join them," Dom said, reading an update on Hato's whereabouts. "We could split into small teams and cover more ground."

Raff had just put a hot tea in front of Dom.

"Recover and have your drink first," Raff suggested. "Quicklips, Pash, Seethe and Hato are already out there with all those recruits."

"Thanks Raff," Dom beamed at him. He took one fast gulp, but then he turned back to Kiddo. "Do you mind? I promise to give some quality time back to you after your shift tonight."

Kid shook his head, not minding at all. "If being part of the search is what you need, that's what you should do. Some of the others will have to come back soon for the club and night patrols anyway."

Dom leaned on Kiddo's shoulder, sweeping in to kiss his cheek before rising from the table.

"Raff," he said in farewell. "Duncan Jr." he added with a salute.

Duncan Jr. blubbed from his bowl, and Raff sighed as Dom left.

"It's alright, I'll drink it," Kiddo told the man guiltily, feeling bad for the wasted tea.

"No, no," Raff smiled. "You didn't want one, and this one has sugar in it." He took the cup away.

Kiddo clapped him on the back. "Thanks for taking care of Dom."

He descended the stairs to the ground level now himself, leaning on a work bench covered in parts and plans.

These plans screamed Trix's influence. She and Sparks had brainstormed more weapon's ideas for Sparks to bring to life.

At the moment they were working on making one of Trix's fatal pulse grenades − which had contributed greatly to the successful fall of more than one snatcher base − into something less conspicuous. The papers in front of him suggested they were experimenting with disguising them within air freshener designs, garage remotes and even sets of charms hanging from dangly earrings.

"Your Kiddoisms especially come out when you're stressed or tired," Sparks waved a hand in front of his eyes.

He absently put his own hand on her hip and drew her closer. He'd come down here especially to be in the same vicinity as her.

"You've been staring at this bench for fifteen minutes," she informed him. "First you were spinning my pen. Then you were chewing your thumb. And after that you were rubbing your temples over and over."

He hadn't even noticed the pen, until she pointed it out, now in his pocket.

"I was just reminding myself never to touch any remotes, earrings or air purifiers in your garage," he answered.

"No, you were just trying not to worry about all the Razes, and the main Raze, who left here on their motorbikes to search out some snatcher dens."

He gave her a begrudging smile. "It did start that way. Until I saw these plans and had something new to fret over."

She let him side-track her from the truth. "You think I'd leave pulse weapons that could take out everyone in the vicinity just lying around?" she asked. "Not with someone like Jeffrey down here all the time. I've even taken to locking away all the c-gars when they're not needed."

"Fair point," he acquiesced, eyeing her large storage cabinets.

Sparks' military contacts had made sure that she had been given sealed, fortress-like chambers to store her weapons in during development. Those cabinets were as fortified as army tanks made into vaults, and were locked down at all times.

"It's almost funny to imagine opening one of those epic cabinets to discover a glorified air freshener on a shelf," he told her. The pen was back in his hand now, twirling in his fingers.

"You'd find more than one air freshener on the shelf," she confided. "Jingle got the United Nations Security Council to officially-unofficially foot the bill for a whole line of them. And they've given approval for us to use their couriers to deliver them wherever in the world the Raze gang might need them."

"Wow ... really?" Kiddo reached to tuck a loose lock of her sharply cropped hair behind her ear.

"Start's been working away on his maps, marking buyer sites and bases they've identified. They just need the time and resources to get around to all of these places," Sparks went on. "So the Wolf might have a much *bigger* organisation than ours, and plans of his own, but we have a *better* organisation, and the potential to do something widescale, if we can co-ordinate it."

Kiddo realised he was still smoothing her hair with one hand, and gripping the pen with the other.

"And you only half heard all of that, didn't you?" she asked affectionately.

He'd wanted a distraction, and had been too distracted to appreciate the distraction she'd offered.

"I'm zoning out into useless mode," he admitted to her then. "I should probably go to work early. Pash won't be able to give Teddy a ride home, so it's better if she leaves before dusk."

"Good idea," Sparks encouraged warmly. "That way my apprentices will take their eyes off you and they'll get BACK ON THE JOB!" she purposely raised her voice.

The sounds of hard work swiftly picked up again after they'd petered out almost unnoticeably.

Kiddo grinned as she took hold of his arms and pulled him away from the bench. She plucked the pen from his fingers, then sent him on his way.

However, his grin dropped and turned into a groan as he crossed the road and peered into the diner.

"What are you doing here?" he asked with exasperation as he stepped through the jingling door. "I'm not in the mood."

Surely a talk with the Wolf was enough. Now a shark too? Narkon peered up from his conversation with Teddy.

The chef had obviously won her over. They were sitting together at the bench like old friends.

"No, what are *you* doing here?" Teddy asked Kiddo. "You don't start for two hours."

"I own this place," Kiddo answered defensively, circling around the counter. "And I'm sending you home early because Pash can't take you."

Narkon sipped at a coffee that appeared much too fancy to have come from the diner. Yet it was in one of the diner's mugs.

"The chef taught me how to make barista style coffee without a machine," Teddy told Kid proudly when she noticed him frowning at the cup. "Look at the foam!"

"I'll get you the machine, if you want it," Kiddo humphed. He tapped his fingers on the benchtop.

Sparks was right, he was definitely on edge – half his mind still on the possible reasons behind Yorak's visit. He felt like he'd swallowed a running motor.

"Yes to the machine, and I want the chef too," Teddy announced. "He said he'll teach me, and anyone who wants to learn, a whole bunch of skills."

"And why would he do that?" Kiddo asked her, seeing as Narkon was still peacefully allowing her to speak on his behalf.

"Well," Teddy replied, wearing a thinking expression. "He would have a new challenge. A better cause." She glanced at Narkon to check, and he nodded for her to go on.

So they'd been working on this together.

"He would be able to help people in the community who need skills for work, for free!"

"Right," Kiddo grunted. "Free, hey."

"Oh yes," Teddy told it to him straight. "He knows you can't afford him."

Kiddo snorted.

"And he'd be happy to teach and manage during the weekend shifts so that you and I could have a break," Teddy finished cheerfully.

Rubbing his brow, Kiddo leaned against the counter. He directed his attention back to Narkon.

"This couldn't turn into a publicity stunt," Kiddo stated flatly. "We can't have the wrong crowds flocking here for the sake of seeing a famous chef."

"They would usually be considered the right crowds," Narkon at last broke his silence – possibly sensing victory. "However, I do understand. You don't want your clients to feel uncomfortable or to lose their sanctuary."

"I don't want people who need the meals and the place to rest to miss out."

Narkon put his mug down. "I can give those exact people an opportunity and a reference that could lead them to stable work. I won't go bandying about my name and broadcasting what I'm doing. I don't need a pat on the back."

"You honestly don't want money either?" Kiddo repeated in disbelief.

"I have plenty. What I need is something worthwhile to do," Narkon answered bluntly. "To wake me up. And I'll take my meals from here as payment."

"But *I* still want full pay," Teddy chimed in. "That hasn't changed."

"You want me to get you a coffee machine, a chef, an early end to your shift, and full pay?" Kiddo asked her sardonically. "You drive a hard bargain."

She beamed. "And in return, you get to keep me."

Kiddo felt the moodiness lift from his brow as he regarded her.

He gave in.

"Deal."

"Yipppeee!" she hurried to bear-hug Narkon – overjoyed for him.

"Such a hugger," Kiddo shook his head, but managed a smile. "And you," he told Narkon, "are sly."

Narkon dabbed his mouth with a napkin. "How so?"

"You gave up on talking to me, and came early to sway my staff in your favour instead," Kiddo surmised.

Narkon shrugged imperturbably. "I was also dropping something off for you."

He bent to pick up a large, slender package that he'd had resting against the counter.

Carefully, the nonchalant chef slid the wrapped parcel to Kiddo.

Eyes narrowed, Kiddo tore the paper open to reveal a poster sized frame.

He paused, taken aback.

"How did you …" he stared at the framed certificate uncertainly. "How did you get this already?"

Narkon appeared gratified to have elicited a reaction. "I'll keep my fame to myself while I'm in here," he said. "But it does come in useful elsewhere. Especially when you really want to make things happen."

Kid released a big breath. "Thank you. You didn't have to."

Narkon was earnest rather than cool and condescending as he answered. "It's something you can be proud of. I can see that. And you said you'd proudly display my signature when it arrived."

Perhaps a few trips into Kiddo's world truly was beneficial for Narkon too. He already seemed more like an actual person than before.

"That was just an excuse," Teddy chuckled, and Kiddo became suspicious again.

"Oh?" Kid raised an eyebrow at her.

"He wanted me to explain the whole situation with our diner and your gang," she explained matter-of-factly.

Narkon held his hands up innocently. "We got talking. I asked her to help me understand what's going on beneath the surface here."

Kiddo rolled his eyes. "It's too much of a long story. A dangerous story."

"Don't worry! I already told it!" Teddy reassured him. "It was easy."

Narkon coughed lightly into his hand.

Kid's heart skipped a beat.

"Teddy," Kiddo said slowly, feeling the colour draining from his face.

He checked that nobody in the booths or at the tables seemed to be listening.

"What exactly did you explain, and how do you know much about it yourself?"

"Let's see," her eyes roamed upward as she tried to remember 'exactly' what she'd explained. "I told him that there's a massive group called the snatchers. They sell poor young people to rich people. But your gang protects everyone. So the snatchers don't like you."

"Alright." Kiddo's knee hit the counter, he was bouncing his leg that furiously. "You covered it."

That wasn't so bad. She did know the fundamentals – which was hard to avoid in the diner, and she'd heard a little in the past from where she volunteered in a homeless shelter sometimes. It was one reason she'd applied to help at Kid's Place.

"Yeah, see? Easy. Done in a few sentences," she took off her apron. "You know, Beef Cake could even show the chef exactly what the snatchers are like to people and to your gang," she said brightly. "He and Dolly were talking to the Dire guys about your fight before your cooking test this week. They said you were trying to save that kid and beat a whole group of snatchers in an alley." She reached over to pat Kiddo on the arm. "They said you were lucky to come out alive, when so many of those snatchers didn't. So good job! You're so cool."

Kiddo's heart was outright racing instead of skipping this time.

Teddy was swivelling her stool around in half circles. Naïve to what it meant – what it *really* meant – for Kiddo to walk away while the snatchers hadn't.

It felt like a glass of icy water had been poured down his collar.

Narkon's gaze shifted from Kiddo to Teddy.

He knew. How could he misinterpret that?

Yet he still wasn't making a speedy exit.

"Teddy, how could Beef Cake and Dolly, or even the Dires, show the chef my fight with the snatchers? How could they have seen it?" Kiddo asked sickly.

He kept his voice low and controlled.

No need to taint the diner with his dread.

That was the point of the diner. To give people a refuge from the dark.

Even now, there was a toddler bouncing up and down on a red booth seat in the far corner – his young parents filming it and laughing. Two older homeless men were playing cards in a booth further down, heckling each other good naturedly. A university student sat at another table, enjoying the late afternoon sun streaming in over her and her books.

Teddy tapped her chin. "Ummmm ... they said they watched it on live stream that morning. Must be a special gang channel, because I never saw any of you guys trending anywhere."

Kiddo closed his eyes for a moment.

He saw visions of his own hand wielding a meat cleaver as if he were a butcher carving up pig carcasses for sale.

Images of deep, rent open tears in snatcher clothes and snatcher skins. Pink layers, sinewy layers, and then bone.

Red spatters flicking against alley walls. Sprays and droplets hitting pavement. And he'd been so careful and precise to make the right hits at the right angles. Keeping his restaurant whites clean.

"Teddy," he said faintly. "Please don't listen to them anymore. And never look at anything they're watching on their phones. You don't need to know these things."

She slid down from her chair, having caught sight of a familiar car pulling in to park at the front of the diner. "Sure," she said naturally.

"No, wait. Teddy," Kiddo stopped her urgently. "I need you to promise me. Don't talk about these things, don't look at them. Never, never, never again show *anyone* that you know anything about any of this at all. Focus on your amazing coffees and on brightening the day of our customers."

She laughed. "Ok, ok, bossy. I promise."

She offered him her pinkie finger, which he knew was like a sacred oath to her. He quickly took it, binding her to her word.

"Now my mum's here to pick me up. Lucky she likes to come so early!"

As light hearted as ever, Teddy skipped across the diner, the bell jingling on the door as she greeted her mother enthusiastically.

Kiddo ignored how mischievous it was that she'd neglected to mention she'd already lined up a lift home. He just stared after her nauseously.

"I could start here today, and make *you* a coffee," Narkon asked after a moment. "You appear rather sapped after that, and you hardly seemed like yourself even before."

Kiddo purposefully stilled his leg from its jumping, straightening from where he leaned.

"Think about this carefully," he told the chef very seriously, gripping the countertop. "The snatchers are not a 'massive group of bullies.' They are a world-wide underground system of human traffickers. They now have a division especially hunting down anyone in the Raze gang. If I'm not in tomorrow, it could be because I'm at a funeral, or because somebody is organising mine."

Kiddo took a deep breath.

"The law knows about, and turns a blind eye to us, because we do things that they can't. But, think about what that means. What Teddy so casually said. Think about what that means we do. What I did, right before the final assessment."

"I won't be joining the Raze gang," Narkon replied decisively, his expression steadfast and stubborn. "I'll be working in a diner that focuses on uplifting the most fragile people in this community. I might learn some things and get ideas I can take back for a similar project in Paris."

Kiddo swallowed. "Then you will need to do the same things I told Teddy to do. After this conversation today, try not to think about anything beyond your job. Don't listen in or look too closely into anything about the snatchers, the Raze gang, or The Hunt for us. Don't talk to anyone about it if they ask."

Narkon was about to reassure him and to obstinately reaffirm his decision, but Kiddo held his hand up to stall him.

"I'm going to give you one final warning, so that you know exactly what kind of world you'll be getting close to,"

Kiddo said. "Because you are luckier than most, and have the choice."

He double checked the other wait staff and diner patrons again. All enjoying and going about their day.

"Many of the people in the Raze gang are snatcher survivors. We came off the streets, from refugee backgrounds, or are from other gangs," Kiddo said quietly.

"The snatchers are just the sellers, they aren't the only problem. The powerful private buyers and enterprises are what create the market." Kiddo grimaced. "My partner, the original Raze, was experimented on in a conglomerate's secret medical research centre. He was sold multiple times. The club and warehouse owner, Hato, got himself and Seethe out from slave labour in a drug den. A mobster tried to buy Seethe again last year to use him as a sex worker. Velvet's brother was exploited for entertainment as a literal gladiator, before he was killed. Pash was snatched from a Mardi Gras parade for being too beautiful, and a potential buyer said they wanted to hang her head on their wall. One of our current mechanic apprentices is a girl we saved from an organ harvesting clinic at a private health centre. She lost one kidney and her uterus before we got to her. Her next surgery was going to be to remove her eyes. She was one of the few 'freshies' intact enough to save from that place."

Kiddo was studying Narkon carefully.

It seemed right that the chef appeared nauseated now himself.

"There are a number of more recent Razes who have been captured, sold and slaughtered. And my partner and I happen to be at the top of the most wanted list," he went on honestly.

"The people who already work here, and most of the patrons, have seen things and know enough from their own experiences. They are aware of exactly what they're on the peripheral of, and what danger lurks in the shadows of their lives. But you come from that blessed middle and upper class part of the world, where these things might just be mentions on the news or an unsolved, apparently isolated case in your local police station's slush pile."

Kiddo put on a smile and waved as the two card players called out their farewells – again without visiting the till.

"If you want to do something worthwhile, you could volunteer at any community centre in the world," Kiddo said finally. "But before you specifically choose to help *here*, it is best if you take some time to decide."

The toddler in the booth was blowing bubbles into his young mother's glass of soft drink. A cook was singing from somewhere in the kitchen. All so incongruous with the picture Kiddo was painting.

For a few moments, there was a heavy silence from the man opposite Kid.

Narkon was, understandably, shaken.

"I'll understand if you choose to walk out right now and not come back," Kiddo broached the silence.

Narkon turned his empty mug in his hands.

"I … am grateful you have trusted me enough to give me the full truth," Narkon managed at last. He was ashen, but still apparently unmovable.

Kiddo cleared his throat. "My friend Jingle checked out everyone I was sharing a kitchen with for the whole course," he admitted. "And she works closely with the military, so they double checked for her. You can never be totally certain, but I've been pretty sure you weren't an enemy from the start."

Narkon gaped.

"It's hard to trust the rich and famous," Kiddo defended. "I was nearly sold off myself to some of the wealthiest people in the world."

"Right," Narkon accepted faintly. "So how about I make that coffee now … and add another one for myself?"

Kiddo raised his eyebrows.

The man truly was not budging.

"I sometimes drink green tea," Kiddo told him. Finally relaxing. "But I choose to be careful, as I unfortunately have normal person problems too. ADHD and epilepsy."

Narkon actually barked out a laugh.

"Of course you do."

The chef stood up from his stool, and Kiddo wondered if somehow *that* had been the last straw.

Perhaps, to a master chef, someone playing it safe with caffeine, medications and symptoms was just too much to tolerate.

"Well, if you don't mind, *I* need another one," Narkon stated. "And then you can start showing me the ropes."

| 13 |

Thirteen

"It hasn't been as busy tonight," one of the waitresses commented as she passed Kiddo, who was balancing the till.

"Mm," he agreed, finishing his count.

His anxiety motor of jitters was still running.

"It's odd," a waiter remarked thoughtfully, pausing in his mopping. "Beef Cake and Dolly didn't swing by. None of the Dires either."

Kiddo noticed he was rubbing his brow repetitively, as if trying to rub away thoughts of foreboding.

Hadn't the day been eventful enough? Surely nothing else could have happened.

"In fact," the first waitress added, "nobody related to *any* gang has been in the diner tonight at all."

Narkon caught the end of the conversation as he left the kitchen, shaking his hands dry.

"Well, it certainly made for a relaxed training session," he stated. "Easing me in on my first shift."

"Sure," the waiter took up his mopping again. "It could be a light night. But it feels a bit off."

Yup. The whole night had felt wrong, without any spare Raze recruits hanging around, and no rough-around-the-edges gangsters making noise.

Kiddo had just started chewing his thumb, increasingly on edge, when his phone started going crazy in his pocket.

The wait staff quieted, sharing glances as Kiddo opened the group chat.

Jingle: all hands on deck ...

Here it came.

Jingle: ... The Hunt has hit the three major gangs.

Pash: wut?! Why?

Pash was back at the club with Hato.

Jingle: unknown. Dom got panic calls from each of the big bosses at the same time.

Tiny: You must be getting too close to the snatcher dens. You've been tracking them since the Wolf crashed Dom and Kid's date.

Flip: good. Make them sweat.

Start: doesn't sound reactive. Sounds well planned, if it all happened at once.

Kiddo wasn't so sure it was a defensive tactic on the Wolf's part either. What if Yorak had deliberately elicited a dramatic response, drawing them off on a search so he could go about business elsewhere?

The Silver Bullet's turf was closest to Hato's base, which was why Beef Cake and the other Bullets often came to Kid's Place.

But The Dires and Hellions were each further out, and at opposite directions. For them to have been hit all at once while the Raze gang were out after Yorak did sound infuriatingly premeditated. Of *course* Yorak had had ulterior motives over lunch.

Jingle: Seethe's group is en route to The Dires. Quicklips' group is arriving at Hellion territory. Dom's group is with the Silver Bullets.

Pash: Hato and I will keep watch around home base in case something fishy's going on.

Sparks: Kiddo and I will taxi patients to the clinic. I'll message the apprentices for help.

Frazzle: Dalee and I will ready. We will call in favours.

Tiny: good luck. Careful guys.

Kiddo glanced up from his phone.

Narkon was frowning with concern. The other two were waiting with bated breaths.

"Got to go," Kiddo said.

"I'll close," the waitress answered hurriedly.

Kid was already vaulting himself over the counter.

Bolting across the road, he saw the roller doors to the garage rolling up so that light spilled out over the street.

Pash, wearing the tough guy look tonight, blew Kiddo a kiss before he flipped his helmet screen down and roared off on a patrol bike.

Sparks tossed Kiddo the keys to a van, already swinging herself up into her own vehicle.

"You meet Dom," she called. "I'll go to Seethe. Jingle's off to assist Quicklips. Some girls are coming back to lend a hand too."

"Got it," he affirmed, rushing to jump into his van's driver seat.

"Oh, and don't drive like a maniac," Sparks yelled out. "We both have medics in the back!"

Kiddo glanced over his shoulder to find three nurses – live-in staff from the clinic, each clutching their medical bags and perching on the bench seats that ran along the sides of the van walls.

Two were wide eyed and mussed, with the look of people who had just been startled awake. The third was an older nurse who still had her hair set in rollers, but who wore a no-nonsense expression that was all business.

"Wow," Kiddo complimented the three of them in surprise. "You guys organised fast. Alright, no driving like a maniac."

He and Sparks pulled out of the garage and took off in different directions.

He tried to ignore the alerts flashing from his phone.

Seethe: casualties. Many injuries.

Seethe: definite Hunt action. Left a damn wolf card at the wrecked gates.

Quicklips: gang house bombed. Will need to take people in.

Kiddo gripped the wheel tightly, his stomach twisting as he turned down the industrial street that The Silver Bullets called home.

"Ohhh shit ..."

Their compound was burnt out, and in some cases, still burning.

An orange, wavering glow illuminated the scene. It was

accompanied by the surging blues and reds of emergency vehicle lights.

Jets of water blasted from the fire department's semi-circle of trucks. They were focusing on the massive heart of the compound, which was in a blazing heap under its expansive, collapsed roof. The showroom had been the Silver Bullets' pride and joy – where they kept all of their hard earned, or sometimes illegitimately acquired cars.

They were auto specialists and racers.

Any Silver Bullets who could still move appeared to be making a scene over there, so that was where Kiddo would start.

The front gates had been obliterated, and Kiddo drove the van in to park beside the ambulances that had arrived, feeling like he was entering a war zone.

"I'll work out who's best to come back with us instead of going with the system," Kiddo told the medics as he parked. "You help the ambos while I do my first trip."

They nodded, faces pinched as they opened the van doors and dispersed.

"Shit, shit, shit," Kiddo muttered to himself.

Nobody who had been at the gate blast needed help. They'd been skipped straight to cremation.

There was a club house still smouldering to the left, and alongside the fire department, Raze recruits were swiftly dragging living Bullets free.

Kiddo didn't pause, but sprinted to where a scuffle had broken out before the main blaze.

"I'm not going with you!" a giant man was shouting into the face of a female police officer. "None of us are!"

He was almost as huge as Hato. He had apparently thrown off two paramedics, and the officer had jumped in to intervene.

The man – covered in ash – hulked over the officer like a crazed soot monster.

She was in turn unphased, but her fingers flickered toward her hip.

Kiddo slipped in between them, catching the man's fist and throwing it backward before it could hit anybody and force a gun to be unholstered.

"You watch yourself," Kid growled into the man's face – making the soot monster focus on him.

"Hey!" the man yelled, wrapping his fist in Kiddo's shirtfront now instead.

"Boss man!" an anguished voice came from the ground nearby.

Beef Cake's voice.

"Boss, that's Kiddo. From the Raze gang."

Kiddo shoved the larger man backward, feeling a flash of anger when he realised that this man was Sora, the head of the Silver Bullets, and that he was causing the greatest scene. But the anger settled slightly when Kid noted the oversized, bleeding lump on Sora's head. His eyes were red and glazed with shock.

He'd just lost their headquarters, and who knew how many members.

"Calm down!" Kiddo instructed Sora sharply. "We're all here to help."

"The Razes can help us." Sora aggressively jabbed a thick finger past Kiddo then. "But the law can get out of here."

"The law is what's going to keep the media out of your faces, and put band-aids on your wounds," the female officer glowered at Sora from behind the barrier that was Kiddo.

"We're not here to arrest anyone," one of the paramedics added reasonably. "We want to get the injured to hospital."

"WE'RE NOT GOING WITH YOU," Sora bellowed, and made to storm forward. "WE'LL GO WITH THE RAZE GANG!"

With everything he had, Kiddo thrust his fist into Sora's stomach. The Bullet boss' own charge added to the force. Like a ton of bricks, the man dropped to his knees and doubled over.

"The Raze gang won't be taking on anyone who's violent to emergency workers," Kiddo told him. "We're not a shelter for unforgivable cases. You'll be left here to rot."

Sora coughed, glassy eyes bulging and disoriented.

"Kid, he didn't mean it – he breathed in too much smoke," Beef Cake pleaded.

Kiddo put his face right in front of Sora's once more. "We can't fit everyone, and we can't take on the most grievously wounded cases. Doctor Daleeah used to work in the exact hospitals your Silver Bullets will be going to anyway."

"Also, the Silver Bullets have been going under the radar for the last two years," the cop added dryly. "So even the police are literally just here to help."

"But if you want to stop us," Kiddo enunciated clearly. "You are hurting anyone you still have left in your gang. They don't need this kind of defensiveness from you now. They need your leadership."

Sora's eyes darted to the Silver Bullets, moaning or shell-shocked all around him.

He was wheezing as he took in Dolly – eyes closed beside Beef Cake. Beef Cake bleeding from a shrapnel wound to his leg. Older members covered in burns. Younger members watching him in fear.

"Now get up, and help me collect anyone with lower risk wounds ... or in sincere and deserving need of Raze protection," Kiddo said. "And stay out of the way of the professionals."

Sora grimaced. He pressed a hand to his eyes for a moment; collecting himself. Then he forced himself up with an effort.

"There are living quarters at the far end of the precinct," he managed to growl at the officer.

The opposite side of the car shop blaze.

"There might be survivors."

She nodded grimly and hurried off to round up a team, speaking into the radio at her shoulder.

The paramedics dashed in to start targeting those who most needed it, while Sora began doing what Kiddo had instructed.

The gang's boss hefted two largely intact people onto his shoulders and started moving back to Kiddo's van.

Kiddo crouched down beside Beef Cake. "Dolly ok?" he asked.

Beef Cake was holding her hand, but her usually bronze skin had a grey tone.

"I dunno, Kid," Beef Cake admitted shakily. "She blacked out."

"Over here, please," Kiddo called to one of the paramedics.

He reached for Beef Cake's belt buckle, and Beef Cake blinked dazedly as Kid pulled the belt free – forcing a new hole in it and fastening it tightly around the gangster's leg, below the knee.

A paramedic rolled Dolly onto her side and Kiddo's gut clenched as he saw shrapnel pieces had hit her in the back too.

"She's going to need to go with them," Kid told Beef Cake when the medic left for a stretcher. "Will you go with them too?"

"No. Beef Cake is one of the ones who *sincerely deserves* to go with the Razes," Sora's grim voice came from behind Kiddo again now.

Beef Cake's face screwed up in anguish. "I'm such a stupid, car thieving hoon."

"He's not meant to be associating with any gang or anyone with a criminal past while he's on probation," Sora said.

"But I have to go with her," Beef Cake held Dolly's hand even tighter between his own bloody, dirty hands.

"She'll have plenty of Bullets around her," Sora told him grimly. "Up you get."

"Tell her you'll see her soon," Kiddo commanded.

And tears made clean tracks through the soot on Beef Cake's cheeks as he told her, and kissed her hand.

He sobbed as Dolly was carted into an ambulance, while Kiddo in turn hoisted Beef Cake up to lean against himself.

"Your van's almost full," Sora told Kiddo. "There's room for Beef Cake in the front."

Kiddo nodded. "You'll stay here until my next trip?"

Sora cast his eyes about at the still chaotic scene. "They need a leader here," he repeated Kid's words gruffly. "I'm awake enough to do that now."

Kiddo's heart broke for the people uttering pained moans from the back of the van, and especially for the silent tears trailing down Beef Cake's cheeks as Kid drove.

He found Daleeah and Frazzle already leading an organised ward room, with their staff preparing those in need of minor surgeries, tending to burns, bandaging abrasions and washing cuts.

Extra bedding had been set up for those who weren't in serious need of help as much as in need of observation, shelter and care.

It was surreal to see Daleeah suturing a wound over a Dire woman's brow, Frazzle setting a Hellion's forearm, and Kiddo himself bringing in Silver Bullets to join under the one roof.

On his second trip Kiddo found battered, lost looking gangsters rolling out Raze recruit camping gear in the training space of the ground level. Hato had also pulled out everything he could find from when they'd housed so many freed youths from the snatcher convention at the very start of the Raze gang's formation.

On his return to the Silver Bullet ruins, he could tell that the urgency was over. Anyone who was going to be found alive had been found. The fire had not spread to any neighbouring buildings or factories. Now it was about sorting out the whole mess ... and damage control.

"So there is *really* no connection to the other two clubs destroyed tonight?" a reporter was asking from where the media had accumulated outside the gates.

The cop from earlier stood behind an older superior who'd arrived on the scene.

"... As I said," the superior officer drawled through his moustache. "It was an unfortunate fuel fire accident that is now under control."

"How can it be a coincidence?" another reporter demanded.

"Isn't it possible that the largest gangs in our city are starting a war?"

"Is it a turf war?"

"A vendetta?"

The moustached officer's voice was nearly monotone with neutrality as he answered. "These three gangs do have vast memberships and connections," he granted. "They have their territories. But they are not characteristically criminally violent and have become less and less entrepreneurial in recent years. They have never had a reason for outright war on each other."

"Wouldn't it still be safe to assume that they've turned on each other now? Who else would specifically target the top gangs in one night?"

The officer sounded bored. "Wouldn't it be safer to say that there would be at least one gang still standing, if that were the case?" he asked. "Why would they all plan to simultaneously attack each other, if it was going to cause a vicious cycle of mutually assured destruction?"

"Then, would you say that people should be locking their

doors against some new terrible threat? A threat that can even take down the longest standing gangs of our city?"

The moustache twitched a little. "We recommend people always lock their doors and practice common sense. But in regards to this particular showroom fire, the community can rest assured, it has been dealt with."

While she stood resolutely blank faced as her superior spoke, Kiddo could feel the eyes of the cop on him. She watched Kiddo give his van keys to Daleeah and Frazzle's weary medics so that they could take it back to base.

She was listening to the official lines, but she knew enough not to buy them. And she was fixing the van number and face of someone who might have answers firmly in her mind.

"You should get in," Kiddo told Sora quietly, as the Bullet limped toward the van. "Meet the other bosses and talk all this over when you've all been patched up."

Sora nodded. "You coming?"

This time Kiddo put a hand on Sora to steady him rather than to shove him.

"There are a few bikes left here, and I plan to chase up one specific rider," Kiddo answered, opening the back door to the van to help ease Sora in.

"Raze and the recruits went scouting through the properties next door to see if they could *Hunt* anyone out," Sora informed him meaningfully. "We never saw any suspicious cars here and we weren't hit by a drive-by. We were hit by specifically, carefully, sneakily placed explosives."

Kiddo frowned. This industrial street was huge. If there

was no 'getaway car', and this had been set up over time, then the attackers might be stowed somewhere in close proximity.

"I'll see you back at Hato's," he told Sora, and closed the door to the van.

| 14 |

Fourteen

Not even Jeffrey was answering his phone, but Kiddo was patient – keeping his eyes peeled as he left the crime scene to search.

It was heavy thumping noises – just audible over the distant sounds of combusting cars, blasts of water and the collapsing infrastructure of the Silver Bullet compound – that drew his attention upward.

There ... fleeting silhouettes were dashing about in a battle across the rooftop of one of the neighbouring factories.

Jogging around the building, Kid found himself a steel ladder running up the factory's wall. He hauled himself up, hand over hand, as fast as he could go.

Then he practically flew up the last few rungs when he saw a snatcher just a metre away, thrusting a knife at a Raze recruit. Kiddo yanked the snatcher back so hard, that the masked figure went reeling and squealing all the way off the roof.

Kid pulled the recruit up and they both slammed into the next masked figure, throwing this one off balance together.

The other recruits were wrapping up their clashes, and they were running out of living snatchers.

"Secure this one!" Kiddo commanded sharply, and two of the recruits pressed in to try to keep the snatcher still.

"Woah!" Dom's voice came from the opposite side of the factory, and Kiddo peered up in a panic.

Dom was faced by the Huntress of the group ... who had just pulled a gun.

She was the last one standing, her back to the edge of the roof, her finger on the trigger. Perhaps she'd decided she'd rather shoot than catch a Raze after all.

"Call 'em off," she hissed.

Dom looked like he'd rolled in charcoal and ash, but his devilish grin was bright. "Who?"

He was edging sideways, trying to draw her gun away from the recruits' side of the roof.

"I'm not afraid to pull this trigger," she warned.

Sure enough, the barrel was following him.

"I didn't assume you would be," Dom told her.

Kiddo nearly died on the spot when a car backfire came from the Bullet's wreckage. He was sure she'd pulled the trigger.

"But if you put that down we'll let both you and your snatcher fellow here live," Dom went on, unruffled.

She snarled, her pointed teeth making her face seem freakish in the still throbbing lights from the emergency vehicles below.

"You'll let us live long enough to tell you whatever you want to know," she spat.

"If you surrender, we really will treat you relatively nicely," he pledged.

"Hunters don't surrender!" she yowled, and fired.

She moved fast, her aim switching to her own snatcher, who immediately stopped struggling in the grips of the recruits.

The Raze recruits jumped back in startled disbelief.

"I suppose snatchers don't get to surrender either, then?" Dom panted.

He'd dived away, but the Huntress was already swinging the barrel back to him.

Kiddo was running forward. Jeffrey and the others were gaping.

But a speedy little blur darted out from behind a chimney and got there faster than any of them could blink.

Two small arms shoved at the Huntress, who stopped aiming to flail in complete surprise.

The Huntress' fangs were hidden as her mouth made a terrified 'o', and she felt her back foot step onto nothingness.

The baby snatcher watched, with her fiery head tilted, as the Huntress' arms pinwheeled, and then the woman disappeared off the side of the roof.

"Well ..." Dom managed – blinking from where he had leaned up on his elbows. "That was a shock."

The baby snatcher turned on him with a fierce glare as he said the word 'shock'.

"Don't overthink it. I owed him," she jabbed a finger toward Kiddo. "And I owed you. Now we're even."

Dom sat up. "A sandwich and a doggy-bag for a life. I

get it. But how in the world do you keep popping up every-where?"

She patted her pockets to make sure she hadn't lost any-thing important in the rush.

"I came with the guys you just killed, *idiot*. They wanted to stay up here for the show, but you wrecked the Huntress' camera during your fight."

Kiddo had stepped closer to Dom. "Would you like to come back with us?" he asked the baby snatcher. "We can help you."

"Yeah right," she rolled her eyes. "I'm outta here."

And Kid's heart jumped into his mouth for a second, as she quickly lowered herself off the side of the roof.

In an instant, she'd gone.

Just as mortified, Jeffrey ran across to peer over, but then he sagged with relief. "Little monkey slid her way down an-other ladder."

"Bloody hell," Dom gaped, flopping down flat and clutch-ing his chest.

The baby snatcher's exit had floored him more than the gun had.

Kiddo stooped down beside him. "You're a wreck."

Dom grinned. "You're beautiful. But we *both* need a shower before getting into that bed of yours. I hate the smell of burning."

Kiddo reached out and pulled Dom up. "The night's not over yet."

When they slunk back to where their bikes waited at the ruins of the Silver Bullet gates, Kiddo wasn't too astonished to see the moustached officer and the female cop waiting for them.

"Raze?" the senior asked, as Dom approached first.

Dom gave a curt nod.

"So *these* are the guys who keep giving me unexplainable paperwork," the cop folded her arms, eyeing them all. "There are messes all over the city. I write them up, then the files get signed off with no chase up permitted. Are all the rumours about the vigilante Raze gang true?"

"It's above your pay grade," the senior growled. "Hush up."

She pursed her lips. But her face told the rest of what was on her mind. Those 'messes all over the city' were always unidentifiable bodies of completely identity stripped snatchers who had clearly been up to no good. They were found in the worst of situations.

Right now detectives were commenting in the background about what explosives had been used. That this definitely hadn't been an accident. Definitely hadn't been a random factory fire. And definitely was the exact same as what had happened at the other gang bases. The opposite to what they'd all just fed to the media.

It was also clear that *definitely* none of those detectives' comments were going to be submitted for general reporting and filing at any precinct.

"The head of The Hunt is here in our city," Dom said plainly. "He's making his presence felt, and doesn't seem to care if your normal world notices his underworld takeover. Maybe it's time you give this need-to-know information to every pay grade. It's going to hurt at every level."

The senior gaped.

"Alright, it's up to you. Pass it on," Dom sighed. He left the conversation, up-righting his bike from where he must have skidded it to a stop.

He mounted it, and patted the seat behind him.

Kiddo was glad to follow him away from the female officer's scrutiny, and the recruits quickly fumbled for their helmets.

Dom swivelled to put his own helmet on Kiddo's head, and flipped the visor down.

"Hold on," he said.

And the recruits all let their bikes roar to life as he did, kicking off and cruising away to deal with the real mayhem that had now been transplanted to their own home.

| 15 |

Fifteen

"At this point, we've lost eighty members," Madam Hellion rasped. She already had the voice of a concert loving chain smoker, but the night's events hadn't helped. "Another hundred are scattered through the city's hospitals and you've got the rest of us in your medical clinic or on your ground floor."

Raff had outdone himself, serving up every kind of drink that a distraught gang boss or weary Raze member might need in the middle of the night.

Kiddo tried not to wince at how much ash the group were leaving around the kitchen table and all over the chairs. Raff would likely diligently tend to it without complaint the moment they were done with the space.

Kiddo himself was leaving dirty condensation marks on his glass of water, and Dom's mug, which he was making an effort to empty this time, had dusty fingerprints on it.

"We were lucky," the Dire boss rumbled. It was hard to tell if his long, lanky hair was salt and pepper coloured or ash covered. "Most of us were out on a joy ride when it hit. We only lost fifty. About the same in injuries. Any we have here in your hospital got hurt in the efforts to save the clubhouse when we got back."

It sounded cold. But the Dires were made up of hundreds of bikers. Objectively speaking, it could have been much worse.

"We'll probably head back there when the police tape comes off. Or even before. It won't take us long to rebuild."

Under the table, Dom entwined his fingers with Kiddo's to stop him from picking at and destroying his thumb.

Sora grimaced. "Should you go back so soon? The same thing could happen."

The Dire boss shrugged with bravado. "We'll be watching. And we'll be going out of our way to track the bastards down alongside the Razes now too."

"Watch you don't lose your best and brightest to the Raze gang," Sora warned darkly. He eyed Sparks, who just so happened to be seated beside Seethe.

Seethe stretched and lazily leaned on Sparks' shoulder. Still proud to have poached such a precious gem from the Bullets.

"Anyone who needs to can stay here as long as they like," Hato rumbled. "The head of the Hunt has made it clear that he won't be doing anything that could prematurely wipe out any Razes. So our base should be safe from bombings at least."

Each of the bosses nodded in thanks.

"Do any of you have an idea why The Hunt would target the gangs of our city?" Dom asked wearily. The bedtime tea had been the last straw – now he just needed the bed.

"We're a bit insulted," he added. "Thought we were their main focus."

Madam Hellion grunted. "You are. The other focus is for their Wolf to control our whole capital."

"The Dires had a visit from a few Hunters, all friendly-like, in the last week," the Dire boss added. He crossed thick arms so that his leather vest creaked. "Said our turf had a new overlord, and we should make sure to pledge ourselves or face the consequences."

"What did you do?" Quicklips grimaced, guessing the answer.

"Well, *I* laughed," Sora scowled.

The consequences had been steep.

"This attack wasn't about us taking sides with the Raze gang," Madam Hellion husked. "It was about us not bowing down to The Hunt. Our territories are our own," she enunciated that very clearly. "However," she stabbed a gnarled, nicotine stained finger into the table. "The Hellions *are* with the Raze gang. If we were on the fence before, we're off it now."

The Dire boss cracked his knuckles. "We've seen the Raze ads on the under-web. Before this I might've considered catching a Raze or two to sell on myself," he said without any shame. "We could've bought ten new bases for the price The Hunt would pay, and your lot visit us regularly enough that we could have tried," he added wryly. "But losing kids so often when the snatcher empire was deeply rooted here was bad for everybody. It hit many of us personally. So we were mostly on your side."

"Just putting it out there," Jingle replied coldly. "But if

you'd tried that, you would've lost more than fifty people and you'd have no club left to rebuild."

The Dire boss smirked. "We did also consider your potential backlash and powerful friends."

"We're not out to catch or buy any Razes," Madam Hellion huffed. "We're not after *that* kind of power. Or risk ... Or debt."

Sora leaned back broodily in his chair. "One of the reasons that it's only snatchers and Hunters who go after you personally, is precisely because of the footage they're always broadcasting of your work. It drives up your price for a reason. Even our youngest and dumbest prefer to watch you streaming rather than taking you on themselves."

The Dire boss pulled his phone out from inside his jacket pocket, opening a message thread. "One of my guys sent me this link at the start of the week. The wagers were going nuts."

He turned his screen around to show them all the end of a fight.

Kiddo in the alley.

Kid's cleaver chopped down into one snatcher's shoulder and neck, before whirling around to land with a thunk in someone else's chest. It had looked like the knife was coming right at the viewers. Clearly that person had been the Hunter, as the bodycam footage died then.

A 'Raze profile' followed the clip, where Kiddo's status and value were outlined like a product description.

He would make a 'prized possession.' He was the 'eleven' who inspired all of the Razes to first unite, causing the take down of an entire base as well as the death of every Top Two at that time. It nearly ended the snatcher economy. He was also the most beloved of the real Raze. A true catch, in every sense of the word.

"So ugly," Kiddo muttered, his knee bouncing. Dom's hand had tightened on his own.

"There's another great one of Flip and the others taking down a base in Finland," the Dire said, scrolling through all of the many, many suggested clips that came up.

Clip after clip of Dom leading the recruits. And an equal number entitled 'Lone Raze'.

"The Finland base was almost as gutted as our capital snatcher base was when you lot were done with it. The Hunt compiled as much footage of the fights as they could salvage before the show was over, and it was *intense*. If I did care about capitalising on that kind of thing, and could afford that absolute minx, Velvet..."

"The clips show that some Razes are more messed up than others," Sora cut in, shooting a glare in Seethe's direction again.

It drew attention to the fact that Seethe was wearing a frighteningly murderous expression as he regarded the Dire boss.

"Some are more gorgeous, skilful or clever. But all are dangerous, and it means that most people will never mess with you guys," Sora finished, now speaking deliberately to the Dire boss.

The Dire lowered his phone, only now reading the room. "I said we're not into that. The people smugglers are a whole other game," he said defensively. "And we'll be fighting them just as hard as the Raze gang are now."

"We have a common enemy," Hato somehow sounded like thunder without raising his voice. It was a low growl. "And we now exist under one roof ... My roof."

The other bosses didn't say a thing. They were grateful, and possibly slightly intimidated, so no heckles rose.

"You have access to our resources and whatever protection we can provide," Hato went on steadily. "We've recently extended the base with a wing of living quarters, but most of our rooms are full of our own recruits, apprentices and nurses. We can only really offer the few spare rooms to yourselves, as the bosses."

"I would love privacy and a bed," Madam Hellion sighed. Ash had settled into the crinkles around her mouth and had joined forces with the thick, smudged liner circling her eyes. "But so many ... different ... people in one space might lead to some tension. I think it's best I'm with my gang."

Sora and the Dire saw the sense in that, and agreed.

"I've organised for emergency portable toileting, shower tents, essentials, and even a whole bunch of phone charging bays to arrive soon," Jingle tapped her nails on the table, still haughty.

Only small flickers and glints hinted that her scrunchy had been covered in golden sparkles before tonight's efforts.

"So no need to descend into dystopian madness down there, and no need to start looting the streets. You'll all be provided for while you get back on your feet," she finished firmly.

Her opinion of their local gangsters had clearly been dropping drastically throughout this conversation.

"We appreciate it," Madam Hellion told them all, taking the cue to rise. "I'll be first in line for the showers."

"Oh, and a bulk delivery of assorted fresh clothes is also on the way," Jingle sniffed huffily, aiming her comment at the Dire as he passed her.

When the bosses had descended to the floor below, Hato exhaled heavily.

"We are going to be overwhelmed by the number of hot-blooded people here," he told them. "Stay as alert as ever, in case an influx into our base was something the Wolf wanted."

"Aside from a free dessert at lunch today, and a power flex over the gangs?" Seethe muttered sourly.

"Man, I hate that guy," Quicklips groaned.

"Your lockers are as secure as possible, right?" Jingle asked Sparks.

Sparks nodded. "Even if someone bulldozed through the garage, it would be nearly impossible for them to break through those cabinets. Only Hato knows my password, and only Kiddo and Dom would be able to guess it if they had to." She grimaced. "But I'm actually more worried about my clients' most exclusive cars, with a bunch of auto addicted Bullets down there, all looking to start a new collection."

Seethe sneered. "I think I want to supervise the recruits again tomorrow. Just so I can be there while the Bullets drool and Sora watches Sparks work."

Dom pushed back his chair to stand, and then paused as if he'd got up too quickly. "Thanks for that," he said drowsily. "My head is pounding."

Aside from everything else that had gone on that night, everyone was slightly taken aback by that admission, and Dom's easy concession to Seethe.

"Go get some rest, Dominic," Hato answered. "Quicklips and I will do the rounds below, and we'll check in on Pash and the medical wing."

Kid rose too, filling a glass and grabbing a couple of pain killers from their first-aid drawer before handing them to Dom.

Dom downed them with a swig.

"Night y'all," he muttered.

And headed up the stairs as if his boots were too heavy to lift.

| 16 |

Sixteen

Kiddo woke to a knock on the bedroom door.

"Yeah?" he yawned.

Dom didn't stir beside him. A tattooed arm was thrown over his eyes to block out the sunlight filtering into the room.

Pash stuck her head inside.

"Frazzle called a family meeting," she said – with much less vivacity than she normally brought to any wake up call. "And Hato seems pissed about whatever it's over. I think it's serious."

Kid sat up, rubbing his face and frowning.

"Frazzle called it?" he asked. "Did Fraz and Daleeah have trouble with the gangs?"

Pash slipped in through the door, shaking her head. "I don't think so. The hoods are all as slow moving as you two this morning. They're taking things hard."

Kiddo peered down at Dom. "He's wiped. Normally he wakes at the first sound, and if he's disoriented, it's with guns blazing."

Pash tentatively took a hold of Dom's wrist and lifted it from where it shielded his eyes.

"Raaaze," she cooed at him. "Time to wake up."

Dom struggled hard to surface from an extremely heavy sleep. He blinked slowly.

"What's up?" he mumbled, trying not to close his eyes again.

There appeared to be no danger of errant fists flying.

Pash took a firmer hold on Dom's wrist and pulled him into a sitting position.

His head lolled backward for a moment.

"Alright, alright," he said grumpily. "You have my attention."

"You need to get dressed and to get down to the kitchen level," Pash explained. "Something's going on. Hato even has Jingle setting up a group call to Trix and to Flip's team."

"Noooope," Dom moaned. "Be gone. No more problems today."

Kid slipped out of bed and started rifling around for clean clothes. He tossed Pash one of his own zip up hoodies for Dom to wear.

"Ugghhhhh. Back, demon," Dom groaned, swatting at Pash when she mercilessly started trying to pull the hoodie around him. "Back, I say."

"This demon is ... helping you," Pash claimed.

Dom finally stood up when Pash stubbornly continued to yank his arms through the sleeves – like stuffing a doll into a new outfit.

"Ok, ok, I'm doing it," he griped. He caught the pants that

Kiddo threw this time. "Putting on my own pants, all by my-self," he muttered.

"Like a big boy," Pash congratulated him proudly. "Though, a shrinking big boy," she grimaced at his sharp angles and jutting hips, handing him a belt.

They washed their faces and brushed their teeth, with Dom still moving like a zombie. He didn't even steal Kid's cologne.

When they made it down to the living level, everyone was already waiting for them.

Tiny, Velvet, Flip and Start were apparently in a train carriage somewhere, listening in from earbuds. There were graduated recruits filling up the seats around them.

Trix's face had the blue light glow of one of Miss Lotus' security rooms, and Blossom could be seen working behind her.

Sparks had also been called up to join them, and Dom and Kiddo sat on either side of her.

Dom promptly leaned his elbows on the table. He put his head in his hands – gingerly avoiding the sore spot Yorak had reminded him of yesterday – and closed his eyes again.

Sparks shared a glance with Kiddo, leaning in to zip Dom's hoodie up warmly over his inked stomach and chest.

"Even Raff has to be here?" Quicklips asked with a light, joking tone. "Doesn't he have to do enough?"

Normally Raff would be on the peripheral of a meeting, just making life work around them.

But Hato didn't show any humour, and Raff was seated at the head of the table, with Frazzle on one side of him, and

Hato on the other. Hato's giant hand was planted firmly on Raff's shoulder.

"What's this about? Did somebody else get roped into shouting Yorak a meal?" Dom asked a little crankily, eyes still shut. "Don't cook him a single thing, Raff."

Hato motioned with his head for Frazzle to speak.

And the doctor was clearly exhausted after the night he'd had at the medical centre, but he also appeared truly upset.

"I must apologise," Frazzle started. "I got email results yesterday, but ... no time to catch up on paperwork of the yesterday evening."

"Results?" Seethe's eyes were narrowed.

"Raze," Frazzle said haltingly. "Your bloods."

Dom opened one eye. "This is the weirdest doctor's follow up I've ever been to. And I spent a portion of my youth in a *lab*."

"Raze ... there was a trace of medications ... we never prescribed you. In your blood," Frazzle said carefully.

The room was quiet.

Kiddo felt his own blood rushing about to try to get to his head.

Dom finally sat up straight with an effort.

"What do you mean, doc?" Pash asked.

Frazzle rubbed his brow. "Seems Raze has been ... ingesting ... increasing doses of medicines," he explained. "He has build-ups of mixed drugs. Their side effects cause brain fog ... confusion. Wandering mind. Tiredness."

"Uhh, wouldn't I remember doing that?" Dom questioned uncertainly. "I haven't been *that* 'foggy,' have I?"

Sparks put her arm around him.

"You were … maybe unconsciously aware …" Frazzle answered him. "You started avoiding the things that made you feel worst."

Dom's eyebrows shot up.

Kiddo swallowed thickly. "Food?" he asked in a low voice.

Frazzle nodded. "These medications were consumed in foods and drinks. Like long term food poisoning."

And now it made sense why Hato's massive hand was gripping Raff's shoulder. Why Raff had been put in a seat in front of all of them.

This was his trial.

Jingle was wide-eyed; confused. "I researched this man. He came recommended by a high ranking military officer. His files were all clean and legitimate. Are you sure he did this?"

Raff didn't lift his gaze from the tabletop. His tranquil expression never wavered.

"This morning I found Frazzle confronting Raff," Hato ground out the words. "Raff was not willing to give Frazzle the breakfast he had prepared for Dominic, which was placed aside from all of the other, individual breakfasts Raff has always made for each of us."

Raff had always carefully labelled or designated each person's dishes – catering to their preferences.

Jingle was breathing heavily, staring at Raff as if he were a disease.

"I took Dominic's food off Raff, and Frazzle tested it," Hato continued gruffly.

"Yes, I checked it over," Frazzle dipped his head. "It had the traces. Heavy traces now, for a stronger reaction."

One cup of tea last night, and Dom had been half knocked out.

"The evidence is quite damning," Raff admitted as calmly as ever. "There's not much I can say for myself."

"There's ... *nothing* you've got to say to defend yourself?" Quicklips gaped in disbelief. "You don't deny it?"

"I don't," Raff answered smoothly. "I'd prefer to be honest than have it beaten out of me."

"Were you coerced? Were you threatened?" Tiny's voice came from the laptop now.

It was hard to believe that the man who folded their washing, who vacuumed their floors, who knew how they took their tea and had memorised their favourite foods, could be a traitor.

Raff shook his head. "I don't have a family that can be used against me, and wasn't forced. I simply switched sides quite early into my work here."

"But ... why?" Quicklips gasped, struggling to come to terms with it.

Even one of the recruits, who fawned over and adored Dom, would make more sense than their reserved housekeeper with a totally clean record.

Raff cleared his throat. "It wasn't personal. I have spent most of my life working closely with leadership in the military and various governments. I never saw progress. I generally saw steps backwards, and I was disillusioned."

His hands were folded in his lap, his voice was level. It was as if he was simply explaining that the fruit had been unsatisfactory at the market.

"When Yorak approached me, I could tell he was someone who would get things done. A widespread, efficient clean-up. And I could help him, simply by weakening one Raze member in particular."

Kiddo had an out of body experience for a moment then.

None of them, least of all himself, had time to register what he was doing, until he was blinking down at Raff's reddening face.

Kiddo had somehow kicked Raff's chair backward so hard that he'd even toppled out of Hato's grip.

Raff's head was thumping repetitively against the floor as Kiddo felt the tendons in the man's neck jumping and straining. Kid's hands were squeezing around Raff's throat as if it were just a tube of toothpaste being brutishly flattened out.

Hato quickly looped an arm around Kiddo and threw him backwards into Quicklips, who held him with restraint, but also reassurance.

Kiddo was almost snarling for breath against Quicklips as Hato righted the chair and slapped Raff back down into it.

Raff was gurgling and coughing now. Too bug-eyed and purple to be composed again.

"I need to know ..." Frazzle continued after a pause, trying to act as if Kiddo hadn't interrupted so spectacularly. "Is anyone else feel sick in the stomach? Drained? Forgetful? Shall I do more tests?"

The others were shaking their heads, and Raff was too, even as he was spluttering.

"Yorak ... only wanted ..." cough "... me to target Raze." Raff wheezed, his eyes watering and bloodshot. "Said if he got one of his pair, the other would follow."

Kiddo growled, and Quicklips held him tighter.

"I guess I prefer it was me," Dom managed. He tried to peer around Quicklips' bicep to draw Kiddo's attention.

"He said it *had* to be you," Raff held his throat. "Raze is especially symbolic. And Kiddo nearly died when the Top Two's drugs interacted with his medications and seizures. We had to be more careful with Kiddo."

"I suppose you were the one who told Yorak about Kiddo's medical history?" Sparks asked venomously.

Raff didn't deny it. "You get one, you eventually get the other," he said resignedly, labouring to get some volume to his raw voice. "I wasn't quick enough upping the doses, and Raze dining away from home threw me off track. In fact, Raze was meant to be lost in the chaos yesterday. I thought they were going to try to get at him when he left here alone to meet the patrollers."

Dom's voice sounded dry. "Maybe they tried. I think my bike skidded out from under me when I got a distance away from here. Could have been sabotage rather than a dizzy spell."

"You *think*?" Hato asked in a low voice.

"All I know is I was on the bike one moment, and off it the next," Dom shrugged it off. "But I'd been slowing for a light already, and I got up with just some holes in my nice button up shirt. I didn't see anyone around, and it was still broad daylight at that point, so it really could have just been Raff's wonderful efforts that took me down."

Raff was frowning, still trying to suck in gulps of air.

Kiddo remembered what it had felt like to try to press that

man's bobbing Adam's apple right through to the rendered floor.

Quicklips felt Kiddo tensing, and held him even tighter.

"Since when do *you* get dizzy spells?" Blossom couldn't help but join the conversation over Trix's shoulder. "Your lab rat days gave you crazy strength and immunity. You didn't find it out of the ordinary?"

"Since I must've been gradually building up a good bank of Raff's remedies," Dom deadpanned. "And I just thought I was stressed."

"What are we supposed to do with someone like this?" Seethe eyed the heaving housekeeper with disgust. "He's confessed. He's not fighting back. But he's a filthy traitor."

"Death penalty?" Flip's voice came from the laptop – somewhat lowered to keep other train riders blissfully unaware.

Velvet was nodding, like she would have made a happily vengeful executioner if she were at home.

"Too cold blooded," Hato negated. "It's not like our usual situation. We're not in the heat of the moment; fighting for our lives against traffickers."

"We're not used to a normal person making such terrible choices," Start commented uncomfortably.

"Send him to the Wolf to deal with," Trix suggested. "He's useless, with his cover blown. Doesn't matter how good his sandwiches are."

Jingle stood up curtly. "No. I'll tell you what we're going to do." She took decisive steps toward the man she had hired.

It horrified her that no matter how highly recommended

a person could be, how innately ordinary and reasonable they were, or how well she had researched their background – you still couldn't completely trust them.

"We're going to send him back to his previous employers. And I'm going to ask that they do what they think best to a person who has poisoned one of their brightest secret agents, while aiding and allying with terrorists. I don't think someone like Raff will do well in jail. If the Wolf does let him live long enough to get there."

And just as fast as Kiddo had acted, Jingle delivered a resounding slap across Raff's face – cracking his head to the side.

Hato didn't move to stop her as she cracked his head back the other way with a returning back hand either.

| 17 |

Seventeen

"What's wrong?"

Kiddo blinked free of his reverie. He paused in his rhythmical kicking against the washing machine he'd seated himself on.

The baby snatcher had pulled herself up onto one of the other laundromat machines, her legs dangling and kicking lightly as if mimicking him.

She was a few washers away, out of reach, but she was watching him curiously.

"I'm just in a bad mood," he told her.

"Oh," she answered. "You're not really doing what most people do in a bad mood. I thought you were sad-staring. Or having a fit. There's rumours that you get those."

He leaned back against the wall, relaxing his legs.

"What should I be doing?"

She shrugged. "Swearing, raging about the place. Banging things. Now that's bad mood stuff."

He wasn't about to admit that aggression *had* been his first course of action.

"Most of the time a person can get over a bad mood without doing those things," he told her.

"Mmmk, then what exactly are you doing? It's so boring here."

Kiddo smiled a little despite himself. "You're the one who followed me to the launderette."

"Chyeah, but last night you guys were finally doing interesting things. I thought my job was getting good."

"Your job isn't the best, you know," Kiddo remarked.

"I know," the baby snatcher sighed, and scooted back to assume a similar posture to Kiddo again. Her legs hardly spilled over the lip of the washer. "I could've been tagged with Velvet. She's my favourite," she said dreamily, as if she were talking about a character on a trading card. "Velvet's so bad-ass. They call her the Somali princess."

Kiddo swallowed how disturbingly desensitised this child was.

"They're wrong," he said quietly. "She's a queen."

"Lots of snatchers say that if they could get someone, they'd go for Start," she mused. "He could strategise away and make your business crazy rich. Or Jingle, because she could hack you into anything. But Velvet, Trix or Sparks would be my choices. I'd be so strong with them at my back."

She slumped, and shot him a dead-pan look. "And yet here I am with you, doing the washing."

"Drying too," Kiddo said.

He didn't want to scare her off with lectures that she was talking about real people. Maybe he could help her to see it with time.

"*Whhhyyy* are you here, washing and drying?" she asked in exasperation. "Did big Hato make you do it, and that's why you're in a bad mood?"

He shook his head. "I stole the ashy sheets, towels and clothes from everyone in Hato's whole complex, of my own free will."

It was why he'd had to take a van again, and why every single machine in the self-serve laundry was working on overtime.

She gaped at him as if he were crazy.

"Listen," he suggested. "What can you hear?"

She crossed her arms. She waited to hear something profound.

"There're only whirring sounds," she stated, pulling a face.

"Exactly," he agreed. "I wanted to do something productive. And I wanted to block everything out."

"Oh," she glanced down sulkily. "You want me to go?"

That was a funny proposal. She would clearly just retreat to a distance from which she could spy on him out of sight once more.

"No," he answered calmly. "But thanks for offering me the space."

She perked up a bit. "So what upset you?"

Kid considered the question for a moment. "You want the absolute truth?"

"Damn straight I do," she huffed. "Nobody else babies me. And I hate liars."

Her face flickered with guilt then, as if that meant she sometimes had to hate herself.

"Alright," Kiddo nodded, staring at his legs. He smoothed his hands over his jeans, rubbing his palms over the crinkles of the denim. "Your boss was hurting someone I love. And he wants to hurt all of the people I love. So *I* want to hurt your boss."

She was silent, her legs stilling.

"Do you ... want to hurt me?"

Kiddo wanted to weep for her.

"I mean, for doing what he says?" She swallowed. "I don't really like doing what he says, you know."

"You are aware that I have hurt snatchers when they attack me or my friends," he said blandly. "But I don't think you are a full snatcher yet. And so far, you haven't hurt us. Just watched us creepily."

She snorted. When her peers had brought up the fact that she wasn't masked yet, it had been a sore point of shame. Yet now she seemed sort of relieved by his answer.

"What happened to your Raze after last night? He was fine when I left you." She of course assumed that Dom was the one that Kid would get most upset over.

"Your boss had someone we trusted putting poisons in his food for a long while," Kiddo said in a dull voice.

She whistled. "Slow. That Wolf works at a snail's pace. Snatchers normally just take care of business."

She scratched her head imperturbably, but her eyes showed some curiosity. Maybe even concern.

"Is he sick now?"

Dom had taken his steady poisoning much better than most of the gang had. Perhaps because of how furious everyone else, and especially Kiddo was, Dom had gone the other way and had tried to be jovial.

Dom had even helped Kiddo to go around the base in a fluster, collecting all the sheets.

Half of Kiddo's wired up brain had been thinking about how the place was going to go to hell, without a housekeeper. But that was the half that was trying to suppress the other whirring, impulsively vengeful side of Kid's brain – which was not helpful right now.

That chaotic, furious side had very nearly overthrown the flustered, hyper-productive side when Dom had needed to lie down after stripping all the sheets from every bed.

But instead of detonating on the spot, Kiddo had sweetly tucked him in, filled a van and left on a mission to be useful.

Kiddo slid forward and crossed to one of the dryers, which had started beeping. He felt the bedding, and was satisfied that it didn't have any damp patches.

He pulled the first cover out.

"Help me with this, will you?" he asked. "I don't want it to touch the floor."

She was hesitant, and he pretended not to notice how warily she approached. Or how out of her depth she was in the face of clean bedding.

"Could you take those corners? We're going to fold it together as a team."

She ducked down to take hold of the opposite end of the cover he held, stepping back so that it stretched out between them.

"Good job," he praised her as she copied him in folding the material in half, long-wise.

"We need to walk closer together, and meet in the middle to do the second half," he advised.

He was careful not to touch her little fingers where they pinched her part of the cover when the two of them stepped toward each other.

"Thanks," he said, finishing the last two folds.

When he pulled out the next one, she automatically stooped to repeat the process.

"This isn't so bad," she admitted after a while.

"You're saving me a lot of time," he let her know. "And I like that you are being so precise."

He re-filled the dryer when it was empty, and let her top the machine up with coins. She was especially chuffed when he got her to be the detergent pourer each time a washer was ready for another cycle.

"Well what the heck do I do with this one?" her cross voice asked after a good stretch of companionable silence.

She was half tangled in a fitted sheet.

"Honestly," Kid grimaced. "I always just bundle those into a ball and hope for the best."

He pushed the towels her way instead and took over with the fitted sheets.

"Boy oh boy," a cheerful voice remarked from the doorway. "You two are going to be balling socks and folding hospital gowns for years."

Dom was leaning against the frame, hands in his hoodie pockets.

"He seems ok to me," the baby snatcher observed Dom clinically. "I've seen him come away from things looking way worse off than this. Sometimes I even felt bad for him."

Dom pulled a grossed out expression; genuinely disturbed. "Exactly *how* long have you been on our tails? It's so scary to imagine you spying on the team or …" he shivered. "My lone patrols."

She, perhaps unconsciously, had shifted positions so that the two of them weren't hemming her in on either side.

"Do the tattoos go all over you?" she asked, changing the topic. "And who do you like more – Kiddo, or Sparks?"

Dom quirked an eyebrow. "I've got the hots for both of them."

"Yeah," the baby snatcher crinkled her nose at a sloppily folded towel and started it again. "But, like, would you say Sparks is your mistress and Kiddo would be your wife?"

"Sparks is always her own, and on her own terms," Dom mused, humouring the child. "And Kid is always mine."

Kiddo managed a wry smile. He chose not to mention that the baby snatcher was probably digging for more Raze profile information.

"So if you were worried about either of them, would you go off and do some washing?" the baby snatcher was nonplussed. "That's one way to stop the Hunters from filming you."

"You've been doing laundry this whole time?" Dom asked.

He shifted from the frame and pulled himself up to sit on a slowly churning dryer. He nestled between a mountain of socks and towers of folded trousers, close to Kiddo.

"That's hours of slaving to my hours of napping."

"The baby snatcher's been working with me," Kiddo replied.

"I'm not a baby," she argued. "And I'm not even a chipped and masked snatcher yet."

Dom pulled Kiddo backwards to lean against the dryer, between Dom's knees. Kid paused his sorting as Dom's arms looped around his shoulders from behind.

"Alriiiight," Dom stretched the word out. "What *do* we call you then? Seeing as 'Annie' went down like a lead balloon."

She tsked at him, unimpressed. But she was thinking about it.

"This doesn't make us friends," she warned.

"Not at all. It's just so I know who to curse when someone's shadowing me next," Dom shrugged against Kid's shoulder blades.

She nodded, as if that was reasonable.

"Rue."

Kid regarded her. "Uh, like a kangaroo bab … joey?"

"No," she rolled her eyes. "Like, my parents rue the day they did it. That's what the snatchers say."

"It's *way* stronger than that," Dom disagreed. "How about … *your enemies will rue the day they ever cross you*," he amended her version dramatically. "I like it. Sucks that we're your enemies, though."

She turned away to put a neat towel on her pile, but they caught the pleased expression on her face.

"I think my parents were snatchers who fooled around against the rules. I was the accident they rued most," she announced matter-of-factly. "Had to keep it secret. Then couldn't even make a profit selling me off privately in case others caught on that they'd had a kid."

Kiddo had often suspected that that could be his own parents' story. But thankfully he had been dumped somewhere that the right system had found him.

"How did you come out of all that alive?" Dom asked – as direct as she always was.

She shrugged. "I was given to the snatcher clinic staff to raise as a helper."

Kiddo shuddered against Dom as he remembered how he'd been examined by the snatcher medical staff when he'd been taken. Their clinicians had viewed him like a scientific specimen. In their own way, they were just as heartless as the abductor snatchers were.

"It was an experiment," she explained. "Because I was the first one the snatchers ever tried to raise from scratch. But the nurses always said I was simple. I'd be too dumb to do much. They decided it was bad to keep me around and encourage snatchers to make families, so they were probably getting ready to write me off. And then they exploded in the base take-down anyway."

The baby snatcher, Rue, laughed at Dom and Kiddo's expressions.

"I hated them," she said, as if that was reassuring. "I only didn't blow up along with them because I made some mistake – like I spilled something on a rich woman in the big show room that day. I was punished pretty bad and was kicked out so I couldn't embarrass anyone again. So there I was, off on the surface wishing they'd all die, when you blew 'em up!" she cackled at the thought.

"You would have been ..." Kiddo swallowed heavily. "About five? Six?"

"Who knows. I don't know when my birthday is." She automatically bent down to open one of the last front load dryers that had now finished, unstuffing it busily.

"So, you fell in with more snatchers who'd been on the surface?" Dom asked. He tried to hide the hollowness to his tone, being casual.

"Well that was easiest." Rue examined a pair of star print ankle socks as if she liked them. They were Sparks'.

Kiddo turned back to finish his own last pile of folding, sharing a glance with Dom.

"If you pick your favourite time of year, and your favourite number," Dom began. "We could celebrate your birthday then from now on."

Rue lowered the starry socks. "People celebrate birthdays with people they're close to. We're not friends. Remember ... *idiot?*" She said it with almost begrudging affection.

Dom slunk down from his perch and pinched some coins from Kiddo's stash for the washers and dryers. He pretended not to notice when Rue quickly stepped out of his way, as if expecting trouble.

Instead, he stood in front of a vending machine at the far end of the long room. The other machines on either side of it sold packets of soap suds and stain remover, but the central one sold bags of chips.

"I'm starting to wish we were," Dom informed Rue. "I think you'd be an awesome friend."

She ran over hastily when she saw him pondering the buttons. "Can I do it?" she asked. "I'll choose!"

She still stood at arm's length, out of reach, but her face lit up when he handed her the coins.

She pressed her palms to the glass and scanned every row before making her selection and feeding the money in.

"You're not simple," Dom commented. "You knew the right coins."

"One thing snatchers know is money. It's basic numbers," she quipped as an orange bag was released from a coil in the top row. "But I can only read baby books."

"And we all know," Dom appeased her as the chips dropped. "You're *not* a baby."

She stuck her hand in the machine and pulled out her packet triumphantly.

"Good choice," Dom complimented her flavour selection, but he stepped back with his hands up when she shoved the bag at him. "I was going to give them to you anyway."

Rue acted offended, though she pocketed the change and kept the chips. "I don't need you to feed me. I swipe myself great food, and it's healthier than this trash."

Kiddo had found that taking fruits and vegetables from shopfront stands had always been the most painless strategy on the streets.

"I just didn't want you to be jealous," Dom confided. "Because I came here with a gift for Kiddo."

She frowned, her eyes searching him for his hidden gift. "Is it because you knew he was in a bad mood?" she asked. "What is it?"

Dom sneakily withdrew something small from his hoodie pocket, and showed it to her in his cupped hands.

She deigned to get close enough to squint at whatever rested on his palm.

"Looks cheap," she criticised.

"Oh, it is," Dom laughed. "I got it online for eight dollars, and it arrived today. I thought it was perfectly timed to become a cheer-up present."

"Why am I the one getting cheered up?" Kiddo enquired. "You're the one who was being drugged."

He felt his face become stony again.

"Why don't you get him a proper one?" Rue asked, ripping open her chips.

"I will one day," Dom straightened. "If he wants one." He approached Kiddo. "Right – close your eyes and hold out your hand."

Kiddo did as he was told, and he felt Dom take hold of his hand; slipping something onto his thumb.

"Ok, ready," Dom announced.

Kiddo blinked down at a thick silver ring now circling his thumb. Its band had a chain around the middle, which spun smoothly when he ran his finger over it.

"Silly," Rue said, crunching away like a spectator. "It's a fidget toy, and you're a grown up."

"A fidget *ring*," Dom corrected her. "You spin your anxieties away instead of chewing off your thumb," he was explaining – before he was muffled against Kiddo; wrapped tightly in Kid's arms.

Dom pulled away just enough to grin audaciously and kiss Kiddo.

"You're welcome," Dom granted.

"You two are so cheesy," Rue grimaced, even though she was the one with cheesy flavouring all over her. "I can hardly watch and stomach my chips."

"It's good for you to see a loving relationship," Dom answered, nose in the air. "Now help us load all this into the van. Kiddo's got to get back, and deal with any quibbling over whose favourite undies are whose, before work."

"Nuh-ah," she held her pockets safely closed to protect her coins, and darted to the door – orange crumbs all over her face. "You got enough work outta me for one day!"

She stuck her tongue out before trotting on her way.

"Just you and me then," Dom amended, but his eyes were soft as he took in how touched Kiddo was by the cheap spinner ring.

"Yet never fear," Dom went on, taking up a pile of hospital linens. "We're training her, like a cat with milk. We'll lure her in, until we just might get to save one stray."

Kiddo made a basket out of the material of his t-shirt, and started filling it with socks. He put the star socks on top.

"No fear?" he asked without looking up.

"None," Dom reassured him.

It was hard to agree with that, when Dom's damaged button up shirt was at the top of the next pile. A reminder of Dom either being dazed by Raff or narrowly avoiding a snatching.

Kiddo felt a light kiss on the back of his neck as Dom passed by.

"Dom," Kiddo said over his shoulder.

"Mmm?"

"Don't forget..."

"What shouldn't I forget?"

"I love you."

There was a chuckle as Dom stepped outside.

"How could I ever forget that?"

| 18 |

Eighteen

Kiddo found Narkon checking a sign taped to the door of 'Kid's Place.'

Narkon seemed smug.

"I only put it up last night, and see how many paper tabs have been taken," he told Kiddo.

It was a completely unpretentious tear off flyer, advertising beginner's classes in the diner's kitchen. It mentioned work place skills and a job reference for hard workers.

Quite a number of tabs that listed the time and date of the first session had been ripped off by interested visitors.

The first session was for the following day – Saturday, in the quieter part of the afternoon.

"It will be so good for these people," Narkon decided.

"So good for you too," Kiddo also decided. "Not to be known from a bar of soap. It could take you down a few pegs."

Narkon followed Kid inside the diner.

"What are you doing here, anyway?" Kiddo asked, nodding at the table staff as he entered with a tinkle from the bell on the door.

"Don't you get tired of asking me that?" Narkon retorted. "I'm here to check exactly what I'll be working with back there, and what space the other chefs will be happy for my small group to work in."

"We have plenty of everything," Kiddo said. "Your students should have all the resources they need. But check away." He made the 'after you' gesture toward the swinging doors, but then felt a bear hug wrap around him from behind the moment he lifted his arms.

"Hey Kid," Teddy said into his back.

"Pash said he's definitely giving you a ride home," Kid told her. "He's going nuts with such a full house over there."

"I'll call and ask for Lady Pash," Teddy bounced on the spot, whipping out her phone. "Lady Pash talks more about photoshoots and other celebrities, because it's between us girls."

Kiddo scratched his head.

Both Pashes were very much Pash either way.

"I noticed it was busy across the street," Narkon commented in an off-hand way, not having budged toward the kitchen at all. "What went on last night?"

A broad shouldered young woman, with a braid down her straight back, turned around from where she'd been waiting at the counter then.

She wore a no-nonsense expression, and even without the badge and uniform, she also wore the assured confidence of a cop.

"I've come here to see if I can clarify that, myself," the female officer interrupted dourly.

"Ugggghhhhhhh," Kiddo groaned. "Can I not just come to the diner to *work?*"

Teddy got off the phone in time to pat him on the back, with no clue as to what was wrong.

"There there, bossy."

"Tell me about the Raze gang and the snatchers," the cop said steadily to Kiddo.

Kiddo rolled his eyes skyward. "Uggggggggggggggggghhhh-hhhhhhhhhhhhhhh."

"Want me to do it, Kid?" Teddy asked. "I do it in just a few sentences, remember? Oh."

She stopped the moment his skyward eyes rolled back to shoot a glare at her.

"Sorry, I pinkie swore," Teddy told the officer.

Then she made the motions of helplessly zipping her lips, and she wandered away to tidy some tables while waiting on Pash.

Kiddo threw a sharp stare at Narkon next, but he lifted his palms innocently too.

"All I read was that the city's gangs have turned on each other," Narkon uttered. "The bulletins say we should be battening down the hatches as gangs go to war."

The cop pursed her lips in irritation. It was the exact opposite to what her superior had outlined at the media briefing.

Kiddo snorted. "Those gangs are flopped about on camping gear on our ground floor, playing cards, arm wrestling or healing. They were targeted for not falling in line with the very groups I told you never to speak about again."

Jeffrey had been sitting on the end of Beef Cake's camper bed, intruding on a video call to Dolly when Kiddo had headed out. A few Hellions had been flirting with Quicklips. And Sora had been trying not to salivate over Sparks' special modifications to a clients' racer. Many of the Dires had done exactly what their boss had speculated about – heading back to their base to see what could be done.

"My colleagues and I know the rumours, and we do a *whole* lot of clean up that tells us those rumours are true," the cop said. "But we don't get answers to certain questions, and particularly dodgy cases are stopped in their tracks without further investigation. It means we can't necessarily do as much as we feel we should ..." she said sombrely.

"When I was a newbie on the force, young people were disappearing all the time. Runaways and problem kids, sure, but to *never* get a trace of them again?" she crinkled her face in disbelief. "Then a couple of years ago, crime and disappearances suddenly plummeted here. Only now is it picking up again, at an incredible rate. So I want to know what's really going on, and I want to work out what officers like myself can do."

"Nope, nope, nope," Kiddo cut her off. "We've done the right thing and talked to your leadership. I'll call you some other Razes to talk to if you want more. I've got things to do."

Narkon was covering his mouth as if in serious thought, but Kiddo was sure he saw a hint of amusement in the chef's eyes.

"Shut up," he told Narkon. "I can only be bothered explaining once in a week. The chef got in before the cop."

"I didn't say a word," Narkon lifted his shoulders. "Though I suppose I was quite fortunate to be served a burger and fries before you brushed me off the first time."

Kiddo wiped agitatedly at the counter.

"Sorry," Kid grunted at the cop. "Please feel free to order something while you wait."

She was seated at a booth and tucking into a well-cooked steak with vegetables when the bell on the door chimed again.

Hato, Seethe and Dom had answered Kiddo's exasperated group message about the police officer. Officer Koa.

Dom winked at Kiddo as he followed Hato in.

The two of them had only recently parted, but that wink was enough to pluck a flicker of a smile from Kid.

Everyone else, however, was apparently rendered speechless.

For a few moments, it was like everyone in the diner had drawn a collective breath. The air was sucked out of the place and all eyes were on Hato, Seethe and Dom as they approached Officer Koa at her table.

Even the complete civvies, who had never been touched by the other world existing so ominously close to theirs, and who had simply stopped by for a nice meal, felt the shift in the energy of the room. They peered at the charismatic newcomers with curiosity.

But for everyone in the know, or even slightly in the know, having so many original Razes, and the true Raze, here in the one space beyond their base, caused a ripple of interest and electricity.

Now Kiddo realised that it could half be attributed to what people might have seen those Razes do, as much as what rumours had been spread.

Hato shared a few words with the cop before she nodded for them to join her.

Hato took up half a booth seat by himself, and the wiry Seethe spread out on the other half beside him. Dom twirled an empty chair around to add to the end of the table so that Koa had the comfort of a clear exit on her side.

"They are *terrifying*," Narkon commented.

"The giant one is basically my dad," Kiddo answered. "You've met Raze, you know he's ok." He paused at Seethe. "I guess the blonde one *is* terrifying."

"Something about him gives me the chills," Narkon shivered.

"Wait until you meet Velvet," Kiddo smirked.

The three 'terrifying' Razes were listening to Koa, and Kiddo was off the hook. He was relieved to leave them to it.

He disappeared into the kitchen to put together a few more steak dishes, choosing the vegetables he knew Hato, Seethe and Dom liked best.

The continuous jingling of the bell at the door, and the rise in raucous volume out there told him that hungry, bored gangsters were also probably piling in from across the road, and their orders would be stacking up soon too.

"Don't cut off a finger while you're on autopilot," Narkon commented, as Kiddo left the steaks to rest for a few moments, and rapidly started chopping peeled potatoes for one of the other chefs.

It was only then that Kiddo, who had been engrossed in his task, realised he'd been rubbing shoulders with the master chef, easily stepping around and sharing the nearest stovetop with Narkon as his neighbour.

"Hey, I graduated your class already," Kiddo reminded him, pausing with the potatoes and plating up his gangs' meals. "You … really took testing out the kitchen to prepare for tomorrow seriously," he added.

Narkon nodded. "I felt bad when I saw how busy it was getting, so I stayed. It's the complete opposite to last night."

There was a steaming line of plated up orders along Narkon's bench, waiting for the harried wait-staff to be back for them.

Kiddo shook his head. "Free labour is always welcome." He balanced the three plates across his arms, checked the coast was clear through the round windows, and backed out the swinging doors.

"Personally prepared," Kid told Dom as he set the iron rich meal down in front of him first.

"That one's got to be mine," Seethe took the plate with the steak that was so rare it was still bleeding. He passed Hato the well done one – similar to how the cop had ordered hers.

Kiddo continued firing out meals and helping the others with theirs, finding that he enjoyed the dance of the busy kitchen with Narkon naturally fitting in beside him.

Of course, in his teacher role, Narkon had never got involved in any more than critiquing and harpooning the cooking of others. But he seemed to be relishing having his sleeves rolled up and being part of the bustle.

General mass production, rather than delivering gourmet delights, did still have its own charm and challenges.

The chef stayed until well after the dinner rush, taking the time to chat to the other chefs.

Kiddo had also been catching glimpses of Koa's conversation, and he'd been noticing that as the discussion became less intense and business-like, two of the three Razes had lost interest – while one had continued to barely break eye contact with the cop.

Dom had been the first one to wander away. He'd sprawled out in Miss Dorris' booth to help her with her crossword.

Seethe had even sauntered off to harry the recruits that had come in. They were sharing a table with a mix of Hellions, Dires and Bullets.

Yet Hato sat opposite Koa with complete concentration, even offering rumbling answers more regularly than he usually would.

It almost had the vibe of … a date.

Kiddo of course chose to be the one to clear that particular booth of its dishes.

"You're lucky I'm being so nice to you, after the amount of times I've had to deal with your snatcher leftovers with no explanation," she was saying.

She shook her fist at him, and while she was stout and undoubtedly powerful, her threatening hand was like someone waving a pebble at a brick wall.

"Very lucky," Hato agreed companionably.

Kiddo accidentally clinked the plates as he lifted them, betraying how flabbergasted he was.

Hato studiously ignored him. But his slightly curved mouth seemed to say: 'that's right, I'm flirting.'

Later, when Kiddo brought them coffees from the brand new, glorious coffee machine that had promptly been added to Kid's Place, Hato even cracked a joke.

"They're not just an invisible gang in our city are they?" Koa was asking.

"You would find them in every major city of the world," Hato answered. "It means we get to travel for work."

"Nice," Koa burst out with a chuckle – being charitable there. "Could be a fun career move."

"You'd have a great boss," Hato shrugged. His deep voice always came off as intimidating, but it was clear he was trying to be light hearted.

"Is it a problem that my own bosses would describe me as annoying?" she nodded her thanks at Kid as he placed her coffee in front of her.

"Means you must really be doing your job."

"Is it a problem that I would never date one of my bosses?"

"That *could* be considered a problem."

This was Hato … bantering?

Kid was turning away from the table with a fuzzy feeling, completely at ease for the first time that day.

Until he saw the baby snatcher, Rue, waving at him frantically from the door.

| 19 |

Nineteen

"Kid?" Hato asked, when he noticed Kiddo had frozen.

The fuzziness had been replaced by a swift sinking sensation in Kiddo's stomach.

He wasn't sure why, but when he'd seen Rue's anxious face, his first instinct had been to scan the diner for Dom.

Seethe loosened the headlock he had around Jeffrey.

"What is it?" he questioned Kiddo, though he was frowning at the sight of the snatcher baby at the window.

"Where's … Raze?" Kiddo asked, instead of answering Seethe's question.

"He went to bring his nanna's car in closer so she didn't have to walk far," Jeffrey answered with a cough. "About a half hour ago."

Seethe straightened. "He said he'd come back in to get her before he left. I was going to go with him."

Miss Dorris wasn't in the diner either.

Kiddo went straight for the door.

"Rue, what's happened?" Kiddo asked.

Her eyes were as wide as saucers and she skittered right

away from him as Seethe, Hato, and even Koa, followed him outside.

"Your boyfriend…" Rue hugged herself and spoke shakily. "I saw him on the ground behind the diner. And an old lady's crying over him."

Kiddo was off in a beat.

He skidded to a stop before he could collide with Miss Dorris, but knelt down the moment he spotted Dom half sitting up against the diner wall.

"Hey Kid…" Dom uttered. He took a long breath, eyes glassy. "Now *here's* the one I'm safe with," he said almost to himself. "Who loves me. Is always helping me."

The lighting wasn't as great behind the diner, but Kiddo could see a graze on Dom's jaw and cheekbone.

"Ouch," Dom puffed as Kiddo hurriedly started checking him over. "M'alright."

Kid couldn't see any blood, but it was impossible to tell if there were bruises or even signs of breaks under all those tattoos.

"Dominic?"

It was all Hato had to say. He had wrapped a ginormous, comforting arm around Miss Dorris, whose stooped figure huddled below his sternum.

"Got no idea what happened," Dom winced, glancing at his shaking palms, which were grazed too.

"No idea?" Seethe asked. He sounded angry, but that was just his way.

"Can't remember," Dom shook his head.

"Raze… Raze was gone so long," Miss Dorris said brittlely.

"I thought maybe he'd told me to meet him outside, and it'd slipped my mind. So I came out to check. But my car was still in its parking spot, and I heard my Raze's voice moaning from back here."

"It's ok. I'm sorry nan," Dom told her affectionately, trying to sound like his usual self.

He swallowed thickly.

"It's a bit funny ... I mean ... I think *I'm* the one who came out in the dark and had a fall after all that."

He actually laughed in disbelief at himself.

"But ... you said ..." Miss Dorris had a wavery catch to her voice that could have broken anyone's heart. "You said you couldn't ... remember who I was when I first saw you."

Dom pulled himself up straighter and reached for her hand. "Miss Dorris, I think I hit my head."

He frowned, sobering and forcing himself back to clarity at the sound of her fear.

"But I promise, my memory is strong enough for the both of us. I won't forget you and I won't let you forget me."

"Why would you have been back here?" Seethe asked slowly. "Miss Dorris' car is in the front carpark."

"Guys, I honestly don't know," Dom sighed. "I mean, I feel like I got beat up. But, I was dizzy and blurry for a while before I could see straight again. I seriously think I just lost a fight with the pavement."

Kiddo noticed Rue squatting behind a dumpster. Her face was wretched.

"Rue, did you see anything?" Kiddo called out to her.

She flinched, as if she wanted to bolt, though she didn't.

"You said my boss was drugging him," she hugged her knees. "Maybe it broke him."

"It's true," Dom glowered. "Who knows how long Raff was lacing my food. Makes sense that I might not react well, and have another dizzy spell when it stops. But my nan doesn't need to hear all this," he added, pouting at her like a sulky child so that she gave him a watery, wobbly smile and patted him on the head.

"I'll take Miss Dorris home," Hato announced.

"Then I'm going too," Seethe asserted.

Whether Dom had been attacked or not, with recent developments it didn't seem like the best idea for a Raze to hit the streets alone right now.

"Thank you … very much. You are both dears," Miss Dorris said faintly, though her voice still quivered. "I have a nice pack of biscuits I've been meaning to open, and two of the loveliest teacups for you to use."

Koa had ranged from serious faced, to intently listening, to softening visibly as she saw the lion-like Seethe and hulking Hato agreeing to dote on Miss Dorris and her cups.

"This is where it's handy to have a cop as a friend," Koa asserted, already scanning the scene with keen eyes. "I might take a look around tonight, and again in the light tomorrow. I'll see if there's a story that can be found here."

Seethe reached out to pull Dom up, but even Dom was surprised by his clumsy stumble as he rose, and his eyes spaced out again for a moment. He fell against Seethe instead of straightening.

"Take him straight to Frazzle and Daleeah," Hato instructed Kiddo stiffly.

"Back door," Seethe added.

Kiddo nodded, slinging Dom's arm over his shoulder.

"Oh my God, I can walk," Dom argued. But he sagged against Kiddo all the same.

Rue was already gone when Kiddo checked again, while Seethe held the back exit to the diner's kitchen open for Kiddo and Dom.

"What on earth happened?" Narkon asked, hurrying over as he saw Kiddo unexpectedly entering from the 'rubbish door,' with Dom propped up against himself.

"No clue," Dom grumbled, sick of admitting it.

"Heads down," Kiddo warned the other kitchen staff.

They went straight back to bustling about the kitchen. They knew it was probably safer not to see things that went on with the Razes.

"Might just be a knock to the head," Kiddo replied, when Narkon refused to be as obediently blind as the others. "He can't remember."

"There's a psychedelic party happening in my skull right now," Dom joked. "Which does suggest I headbutted some cement."

Kiddo winced sympathetically. Light shows often happened to him before a seizure.

"Let me help you across the street," Narkon untied his apron and slipped it over his head.

The older man was slightly taller than Kiddo and Dom, but he was trim and fit. He would be a good balance on Dom's other side.

"Thanks," Kiddo accepted gruffly. "But not across the street. Under it."

Narkon blinked at him. Possibly wondering if Kiddo had also hit his head at some point.

"He's ashamed of me," Dom closed his eyes sadly. "Doesn't want all the tough guys out there to see my fragile state."

He was being theatrical, but the second part was also the truth of it.

It might make people nervous to see their vigilante hero in a vulnerable state. And it could give any Raze Hunters ideas if they caught wind of it.

"Could you move those crates?" Kiddo asked Narkon.

Narkon humoured him, and slid a stack of unused crates out of a seemingly useless corner that had been hemmed in on either side by fridges.

The chef paused in surprise when he saw that there was a large square shape in the lino flooring there.

"That square lifts, like a trap door," Dom divulged.

The kitchen staff were all studiously doing anything other than watching them right now.

Narkon poked his finger into a seemingly innocent hole in one part of the lino square, and watched in fascination as the whole corner of flooring lifted out to reveal empty space below.

Or, not empty. There were emergency lights illuminating the dimness below, and they appeared to stretch onward for a great distance.

It was a secret safety tunnel, inspired by Miss Lotus' underground network in Tokyo.

"I guess it's worth you knowing about it," Kiddo told the chef. "I'll consider letting a few others know that it could serve for evacuating people if the need ever arose."

"We would just use the doors and windows if there was a fire," Narkon frowned, peering into the tunnel. He shuffled forward to lower himself in, like a swimmer levering his body into a pool.

He checked over his shoulder when Kiddo was silent.

"Kid meant if the threat was *trapping* you in the diner," Dom supplied. "Or trying to murder you."

Narkon's face hardened as he remembered the photos of the blown up gang houses from the papers.

It wasn't a great distance to climb down before his feet touched a ramp that lowered him steadily into the underground passage, and Narkon lifted his arms up to take Dom's weight as Kiddo eased them both in.

When Narkon had helped Dom to duck and descend far enough that they could straighten up, Kid crouched and pulled the false lino square back into place. Then he edged downward and got back into position under Dom's arm.

"Where does this lead?" Narkon asked as the ramp levelled out to a flat walkway, and the tunnel doubled them back by curving around. "It seems to go on for quite a while."

"We're under the diner now. The next ramp offshoot takes you out to a safe distance away down the street," Kid explained. "After that it connects to the ground floor of our base, and then further on there's a ramp that gets you into the medical centre."

"I see why you kept it secret," Narkon understood.

"Imagine how much fun you'd have if you could use it to get in and out of work," Dom mused drowsily. "Everyone would wonder how you kept popping up and vanishing."

"Dom, are your eyes open?" Kiddo asked, trying to squint through the dimness. He'd realised that Dom had started to allow Narkon and Kiddo to almost completely carry him. His head hung forward and it sounded like his feet were dragging.

"Nope."

"Open them."

There was a long suffering sigh. "There are so many bursting bright lights either way. It's annoying."

Kiddo couldn't help fretting and moving them on even faster. "I've seen you take many blows to the head, and bounce back better than this. All I want is eyes open."

"I must've hit the same spot that never quite heals. Maybe this time a self-inflicted head knock was too much for me to take. Too embarrassing," Dom groaned. "Slow down, I'm getting motion sickness."

"How is that embarrassing?" Kiddo puffed. They were approaching the street exit ramp. "And I'm not convinced you simply fell."

"I'm sure I'd remember being jumped," Dom remarked. "Though it happens so often, it does all blur together."

"Not this exit, the next one," Kiddo told Narkon, guiding them on until they reached the last ramp. "Can you wait here with him? I want to see if I can find Fraz or Daleeah first."

Kiddo pushed against what seemed to be a wall panel this time, inching it open so that a crack of white light spilled into the tunnel from the clinic.

"So bright," Dom complained balefully, resting his head against Narkon.

Kiddo peered through the gap and appeared satisfied after a few moments, opening it wider and slithering out.

"I'll be back."

Kiddo surfaced in the quiet waiting room of the clinic. Both Daleeah and Frazzle's offices were empty at this time, but it was likely one of them would still be doing the rounds in the ward, with such a high number of patients.

He didn't want to get caught with any stir crazy or enthusiastic gangsters right then, so he watched from behind the door to the ward until Frazzle could be seen, withdrawing from one of the curtained sections.

Frazzle was always as edgy as Kiddo was, so the doctor jumped and noticed right away when Kiddo pushed over a 'wet floor' sign near the ward entrance.

"Hey Fraz," Kiddo whispered when Frazzle approached to fix the sign.

Frazzle at once straightened and slipped out of the ward to join Kiddo in the hallway.

"Is all alright?" Frazzle asked.

"Not really," Kid said nervously. "Something's up with Dom again. Can you check him out?"

Dom could be heard chatting away to Narkon without a shred of subtlety as Kid and Frazzle neared the tunnel entrance.

"I think Kiddo is such a good role model for you," Dom was telling the first class chef.

"You don't think I might make the good role model for him?" Narkon questioned in return.

"Hey, let's do a quick memory test," Dom suggested. Then he prattled off some phrases Kiddo had heard him use in Tokyo. "Did I forget my Japanese?"

Narkon's voice was easy-going and level. "I'm not sure. I don't speak Japanese."

"Here, how's my French?" This time Dom spouted some entirely unfamiliar phrases.

"If you ever knew French," Narkon said dryly. "It appears you've forgotten it."

"Kiddo!" Dom greeted Kid, squinting as he let in the light. "I never knew French, right?"

"Is your nose bleeding?" Kiddo asked anxiously in return. He hadn't been able to see it before.

Dom dabbed at his nose in bewilderment. "Must've started in the tunnel."

He frowned and shielded his eyes as he was brought into Frazzle's office.

Narkon and Kiddo set him on Frazzle's examination bed, and he laid down pliantly.

Kiddo rushed to blot what had become dried blood from Dom's nose with a wet paper towel while he told Frazzle all that he knew. Then he tended to the abrasions on Dom's hands and face.

"Short memory loss," Frazzle repeated to himself. "Did you be sick?" he asked Dom.

Dom huffed from the bed. "I would never waste Kiddo's steak."

So he remembered dinner. It was just the event itself that he'd lost.

"He has a headache," Narkon added, as Frazzle checked Dom's eyes and ears.

"*Splitting* headache," Dom interjected. "How'd you know?"

"The bright lights you're seeing. Sound like a migraine," Narkon told him.

"Memory, headache, unbalanced, drugged so recently," Frazzle listed. "Nose bleed."

Narkon lifted his eyebrows. "Drugged? You really asked the impossible when you told me to turn a blind eye to your world," he told Kiddo dryly. "It's so dramatic."

Frazzle unzipped the hoodie that Pash had forced Dom into that morning. He briskly tapped Dom's colourful ribs and felt around for signs of an attack. Then he pushed Dom to sit up for an inspection of his arms and back.

"Can't see much beyond dragons and fishes," Frazzle pondered.

"Koi," Dom corrected, slumping down again.

Narkon had been wincing at the old burn marks twisting around Dom from each of the dragons' jaws.

"Hand grazes, and on elbows, goes more with fall theory," Frazzle went on.

"Knew it," Dom said despondently. "Miss Dorris will need to walk *me* out to the car from now on."

"But muscle pains can go with attack theory," Frazzle tapped his chin. "Hard to tell."

"Muscle pain?" Kiddo asked.

"He flinches and is … tightly bunchy in shoulders and arms," Frazzle explained. "Right where snatchers might grip and hold victims down."

"Your fingers are cold, I'm pretty tense, and you aren't gentle," Dom returned, pulling the hoodie back around himself and rolling to face them.

"Face grazes could be head held to gravel," Frazzle considered.

"It would suck if it *was* an ambush," Dom moped, letting Kid zip him back up. "Seeing as there are no new marks on my knuckles. All I've got are playground grazes."

He was glum that he hadn't got in any punches against assailants they weren't sure existed, and also glum that he might have alternatively had a senile moment – even if it had been brought on as a side effect.

Frazzle started probing Dom's scalp then, feeling for bumps. But he paused when Dom hissed with pain as Frazzle's fingertips touched the sore spot on the side of Dom's head.

"Strange," Frazzle commented. "Head injury is opposite side to face grazes."

"Maybe I bounced?" Dom joked. "Thank goodness there're no cameras out there yet. It's sounding more and more like I'm lucky not to remember."

Kiddo had already firmly put cameras for the back of the diner onto his mental to-do list.

"You didn't bounce," Kid reassured Dom tolerantly. "Remember you have that spot that you must keep knocking."

"Whether all this is caused by dizzy collapses, by knocks, or by attack, we do head scans," Frazzle decided. "Is too soon after last poisonings for a blood test to pick up much new."

Dom scrunched his face. "But I don't really want to move," he said honestly.

"I do the moving for you," Frazzle told him.

The doctor left his office for a moment, making some

noises in the waiting room, and then returned with a wheelchair.

Dom eyed it with distaste.

"Nobody will see, I push you the quiet way," Frazzle reassured him. "It's ok."

"This week just gets better and better," Dom grimaced.

| 20 |

Twenty

Kiddo sat against Frazzle's desk and scuffed his shoe against the carpet. He was twisting the ring Dom had so recently given him, instead of gnawing on his thumb.

"Thanks for hanging around," Kiddo said at last, casting a glance toward Narkon.

The chef was seated in the office consult chair, as composed as ever.

"Your calm attitude has probably kept me from losing my head," Kiddo added.

Narkon exhaled a short burst of air. "You all seem perfectly capable of keeping your heads in extreme situations."

Kid lowered his eyes. "Not when it comes to him."

He remembered Dom against the brick wall, dazedly saying something so similar to his sleepy sweet-talking.

As if Dom had been waiting for Kid to save him.

Now here's *the one I'm safe with. Who loves me. Is always helping me.*

"You're doing great," Narkon disagreed. "You're doing great things in many regards."

Kiddo managed a half smile. "Like being a good role model to you?" he recalled Dom's statement to the senior chef now too.

"Actually," Narkon crossed one leg over the other. "I think Raze got that one right. He meant that you're having a good effect on me."

"Oh?" Kiddo asked, stilling his spinning of the ring.

"I've felt more alive and useful in this last week, than I have in years," Narkon confessed thoughtfully. "It has been invigorating to be with such passionate, selfless people. And to be firmly in reality. Even if it is a reality I never saw coming, and a reality I very much hope your friends and yourself can change."

Kiddo was stumped.

"I've found myself facing each day with interest, rather than with a sort of aloof numbness that had crept up on me," Narkon added. "I rush away from the academy so that I can see what has developed at Kid's Place, rather than so that I can simply escape back to an empty apartment with monotonous nights."

Kiddo rubbed his forehead. "I'm sorry it was becoming like that for you."

Narkon chuckled. "What a tiny problem, in the face of all the other problems I've been learning about. And you guessed correctly, on your final assessment day, when you accused me of being bored."

Kiddo blanched as he considered how belligerently he had been behaving toward Narkon.

"Any problem that has an effect on us is a legitimate problem, no matter how it compares to others," Kiddo answered.

"But I'm glad that you were fed up enough to be led astray from your kitchens and into mine."

There was a heavy knock on the door, and after a moment, Hato was filling the room with his huge presence.

Hato's dark eyes took in the fact that Dom and Frazzle weren't in, while Kiddo and his new chef were having a bonding moment.

"We haven't met." Hato stepped forward and extended his hand. "You're Kid's cook?"

Narkon reached out to shake Hato's massive hand firmly. "I am."

"Hato, this is Narkon," Kiddo informed him. 'The famous chef,' and 'the trainer who gave me hell' were the unnecessary words left unsaid.

Hato's heavy brow raised almost imperceptibly. Yet he took the news in his stride, despite the fact that Kiddo hadn't had a chance to fill Hato in on any of Narkon's progress from disliked mentor to respected colleague.

"It makes most sense for Kiddo's adopted father to wait with him," Narkon smiled at all of the unspoken messages that had passed between them. "And I have a big day ahead in Kid's Place tomorrow." The chef rose and motioned for Hato to fill his seat. "But I'm glad to meet you, and hope all is well with Raze."

He headed for the door.

"Narkon," Kiddo stopped him. "Thank you. Again." He cleared his throat. "And, for the sake of continuity for normal people in the diner, could you return via the tunnel and trap-door?"

Narkon nodded and gave a short, quiet laugh. He closed the office door behind him.

"Seems dependable," Hato commented, lowering himself into the chair that Narkon has just vacated. It creaked slightly as he squeezed himself into it.

Kiddo twisted the chain on his ring. "Dom deteriorated a bit in the tunnel. Narkon was smooth the whole time. It did help."

"What did the doc say?" Hato asked.

Kid bit his lip. "Too hard to tell if the injuries and symptoms are from an assault or an accident. They're doing scans."

"Poor Dominic," Hato replied flatly. "Can't catch a break."

Kid picked up a plastic respiratory system model on Frazzle's desk. "Hopefully your girlfriend can give us some answers tomorrow," he said casually.

"*Officer* Koa," Hato replied with her title pointedly, "was describing that there are many on the force who would want to assist us."

Kiddo hastily put the model down when the plastic lungs clacked against the wobbly heart. "That sounds hopeful," he conceded. "But it was seeing you show remote interest in someone that was the highlight of my night."

"Mine too," Hato admitted.

They both turned toward the door when Frazzle at last wheeled Dom back in. And Dom was leaning an elbow on the arm rest, his forehead in his hand.

"I'll just stay here on this office bed tonight," Dom announced tiredly. "Can't be bothered with stairs. Certainly can't be bothered being wheeled through camped recruits and gangsters."

"Is it alright to move him around doc?" Hato asked Frazzle.

Frazzle's expression was one of consternation, but he nodded. "Going to get opinions on scans and we re-do them to compare after time. Can't do much more tonight."

"Why the second opinion?" Kiddo asked quickly. "Are you worried Raff caused lasting damage?"

Frazzle pushed some pain killers into Dom's hand, and fetched him a plastic cup of water from the bubbler in the waiting room. "Neurological symptoms of head trauma are there. But others can check the white matter again, to be safe, before I guess."

"Mmm, pills-pills-pills, down the hatch," Dom sing-songed without cheer. He downed the cup.

"Alright," Hato stood, nearly making the chair buckle as he pushed up. "In the meantime, your own room is best for resting, Dominic."

Dom blinked as Hato suddenly loomed over him.

Hato took hold of one of Dom's wrists, stooping down as he carefully pulled Dom up and then over his broad back.

It was a seamless motion, as if Hato was a war hero used to carrying wounded comrades out of battle – hoisting his fallen soldier into a fire carry over both shoulders.

"Wow," Dom managed. "Now I know what it's like to be a giant's scarf."

But he relaxed right into it, nestling in and loosening up as if he were happy to dangle and nap during the ride.

Hato was cautious, and effortless, in carrying Dom's languid body out as secretly as possible from the clinic to the warehouse's fire escape.

Jingle might get a surprise if she checked who had set off her sensors and saw the three of them making their way up to the rooftop. But then again, with their gang, she might not be surprised at all.

Kiddo held the rooftop door open and guided Hato through the library and down to the bedroom level so that they didn't accidentally add any more head knocks to the abnormally quiet and compliant Dom.

Hato only paused, taken aback, when he had gently lowered Dom onto the bed, and Dom caught the big man's hand before he could withdraw it.

"Thanks Hato," Dom told him seriously. "I much prefer the privacy of sleeping here."

Hato nodded, only taking his hand back so that he could reach into his pocket and take something out to give to Dom.

Dom's pale face brightened. "That's not your usual style."

"Not normally," Hato acquiesced. "Miss Dorris wanted to send you home a reminder of her."

Hato was holding a glittering peacock brooch, and Dom took it as if it was the most precious thing he'd ever been given.

"It must have been so confusing for her," Dom said regretfully. "She would have questioned if she'd made up her memories of us."

He placed the brooch on Kiddo's bedside drawer where he could see it.

"She was more worried for you than for herself," Hato

moved to the door. "But Seethe and I make for great company. She was cheered up in the end."

"You … and … *Seethe* make for great company?" Dom rubbed his temples. "What universe am I in? Did I hit myself into a Dorothy in Oz sort of scenario?"

Hato gave a wisp of a smile, hand on the doorknob. "We even made sure her window was locked. Which it hadn't been."

"There we go, back in the normal world," Dom puffed with relief. He put an arm over his eyes.

"Get some sleep," Hato instructed, before closing the door behind him.

| 21 |

Twenty One

Sparks: Kiddo, don't freak out. He's down here.

Kiddo had of course freaked out when he'd woken to a Dom-less bed.

Jingle: also, Kiddo, don't freak out about the base either. I've decided to hire some rescues from the sperm slavers and the surrogate mothers farm we liberated last year. They hate the snatchers too much to ever think the Wolf could make a great new leader.

Kiddo rubbed his eyes. At least today was starting off with better news.

Kid: thanks guys.

He showered, and with a jolt of guilt – made sure Duncan Jr. was fed. Then he went about making two slices of toast. He spread a thick layer of crunchy peanut butter right to the edges of the crusts for both.

Kid munched on his own slice as he descended to the ground level, and put the second slice in Dom's mouth when he found him on the edge of the training space.

Dom automatically accepted the toast, chewing away with pleasure. He was seated on the bonnet of an old Jeep Sparks had been meaning to make over, and Quicklips was leaning next to him. Together they watched a mix of the recruits and assorted young gangsters running about in a war game that Quicklips had set up. Camper beds and sleeping bags had been dragged to the perimeter to make room.

"Is that …?" Kiddo did a double take, his own eyes on Sparks' side of the ground level.

"Yup," Dom nodded, without needing to check what had surprised Kid.

"That's seriously …"

"Yeah," Dom agreed. "She said she came to check if I was alive, but I think she really came as an excuse to meet Sparks."

Rue was passing Sparks the tools that the mechanic-ess requested, with the apprentices pointing out the right ones to the baby snatcher.

"Cat with milk," Dom said with satisfaction. "Building trust."

Kiddo dusted the crumbs from his hands. "Why didn't you stay in bed after such a big night? I thought you'd need a sleep in."

Dom pulled a face.

"He had bad dreams," Quicklips provided Kiddo with the answer, before he tutted and stomped away to bellow at the recruits.

"JEFFREY, EVEN BEEF CAKE COULD CATCH YOU RIGHT NOW, AND HE HAS A SHRAPNEL HOLE IN HIS LEG!"

"*Nightmares*," Dom corrected, after lowering his hands from his ears. "Vivid, awful nightmares."

"You should have woken me," Kiddo said sympathetically. "What were they about?"

"Arrrrgghhh," Dom stretched stiffly and shook his head gingerly at the memory. "All my friends were gone. You'd all been taken away from me, and I could barely remember your faces or names, so I couldn't find you. You'd been replaced by the Wolf." He shuddered. "I think it's because I was so sad about worrying Miss Dorris last night, my brain put me in her muddled shoes. And now I'm even sadder for her, and more horrified by the idea of Yorak taking you all away."

Kiddo squeezed Dom's leg. "How do you feel today, apart from all of that?"

Dom grimaced. "I feel like I danced with the sidewalk. But, like I told Daleeah, Hato, every Raze gang member under this roof, and even *Tiny* sliding into my DMs, I'm alright."

A head of fluffy red hair bobbed around the other side of the Jeep's bonnet then, and Rue flopped her arms up over the hood – her face grumpy.

"Did Sparks get sick of you?" Dom jibed the baby snatcher, becoming more playful at once.

"Don't be silly," Rue rolled her eyes. "Sparks isn't like that. She looks out for us girls."

Many of the apprentice mechanics were female, it was true.

"She's pretty much the coolest," Dom agreed.

"She's so smart," Rue added crankily. A little thump suggested she'd kicked the thick front tyre.

"She's extremely clever, and she works hard to be that

way. But, does that upset you?" Kiddo asked curiously. "What made you leave them over there?"

"I'm not *upset*." She scowled, but her face had reddened, either because she was mad or embarrassed. "I just didn't want to do what they were doing next."

Kiddo peered over to where Sparks had rolled out some paperwork.

"They're reading through something boring." There was another thump from the tyre. "But I sounded out the first word of the title wrong, so what's the point of hanging around for the rest?"

"Good on you for having a go at sounding it out," Dom congratulated her.

Rue huffed. "But one of the apprentices told me the word is said like 'auto', and that doesn't match up to what I got. I mean 'a' is supposed to make the apple sound."

She'd taken the apprentice's feedback very personally. It had flawed her whole reading sounds system on the first try.

"That was a very hard word to start on," Kiddo acknowledged. "Some words have slightly different sounds when the letters are combined in certain ways. A lot of people could be tricked by that."

She sniffed, eyes down on the bonnet and mouth curving downward too. She seemed devastated that she'd messed up in front of others.

"It's great you made the mistake," Dom assured her. "We remember mistakes and learn from them."

"Yeah, I learned that I won't be doing that again," she

sulked. She would avoid failure at all costs at this rate. "I'll never be able to get a job, because I'm simple."

"Most times your strategy to use the sounds of the letters will get you through," Dom disagreed. "I bet you could have read other words in Sparks' document, just by using your trick."

He wrote a word in the dust on the car.

She glowered at it for a moment, but her eyes did lose some of their fire when she saw that maybe she could string the letters together into a word she'd heard before.

"C – o – n – t – r – a – c – t," she sounded it out haltingly. "Contract?" she asked hopefully.

"Nice work," Dom grinned. He wrote another word in the dust.

She sounded this one out in her head, and they waited patiently as she thought it through and pieced it together to make something she was familiar with.

"Motor?" she tested it out loud.

Dom lifted his palm, and without a pause she slapped it in a high five with a gleeful hoot.

"You know, Hato did a bit of schooling as a kid before he hit the streets, and he taught me what he'd learned about reading by using sounds too," Dom revealed. "You'll get faster and faster the more that you do it. You can try signs, ads, billboards, anything. And if the word you get doesn't make sense, at least you're still practising your letters on sight."

Now she was doing a happy jiggle; enthusiastic again, but she stopped when a slip of paper flitted from her pocket. She rapidly patted at her pocket to make sure nothing else was ready to fall out. As if she had important treasures in there.

"Is that one of the tabs from the sign at the diner?" Kiddo asked her with interest. "You wanted to take the new chef's class today?"

"I heard some people talking about it," she closed off a little again, trying to be offhand. "I don't actually want to be a dummy with no job when I grow up. But I decided reading recipes would be hard."

Dom and Kiddo shared a glance. Both glad that she hadn't assumed her only career pathway was to snatch.

"Even reading the word recipe is hard," Dom joked, and showed her how it looked in the dust. "But you're not afraid of much, so I think you could have a go and learn from anything that doesn't work."

Kid straightened up. "I want to head to the diner and check on how the chef does with his new students anyway. Why don't you come over and just see what the class looks like?"

She considered it.

"I might as well just see."

Kiddo turned to Dom. "You, take it easy."

Dom turned to Rue. "You, make my dinner."

"You can't order me around, idiot," she retorted teasingly. Then she narrowed her eyes. "Would you really eat something I made?"

"Hmmmm," he mused, leaning in. "I'm certain Kiddo will end up helping you closely, because you've got him wrapped around your little finger. So I'm sure it'll be safe."

She chortled. "You're on then," she told him, already dashing away.

"Watch the road," Kiddo warned, jogging to catch up with her.

"Yes, daaaaad," she cackled again. And beat him to the diner door.

| 22 |

Twenty Two

While they had started off as a nervous bunch, with Narkon rigidly going over the safety and hygiene rules, the group of very mixed class attendees had soon relaxed into the process.

Narkon was a completely different teacher in a laid back kitchen setting. Even Kiddo had enjoyed the calm explanations and guided steps that the chef had talked his class through. It had been therapeutic.

Soon there had been a jumpy gangster, a homeless woman, a few random young hoods, the nervous waitress who had stood up for Kid to Narkon, the university student who liked the sun on her books, and the young father Kiddo had noticed earlier in the week, all struggling away with mixing their clumpy ingredients into pizza dough.

However nobody relished making homemade pizza bases quite as much as Rue, who stole a new piece of Kiddo's heart each time she turned to him for a measurement, a clarification or approval.

She joyfully rolled and pounded her dough at Kiddo's side,

and watched first Narkon and then Kiddo modelling how to spread the sauce with a ladle. Her own growing circles of smooth sauce appeared to mesmerise her.

She puffed away at the grater, taking Kiddo's advice on how to keep her little fingertips safe, and then she made it snow with cheese pieces all over her rounded base.

When the other students took their ready pizzas out to eat the rewards of their efforts in the diner, Rue and Kiddo kept going with Narkon. They prepared enough batches of dough, and enough toppings to put pizzas on the specials board for the night.

"You're much more focused than Dom at chopping," Kiddo complimented her. "I'm less worried that you'll lose a digit."

"Dom ... Raze ..." she said thoughtfully, as she slowly sliced her way through a salami, tucking her fingers attentively. "What's his favourite topping?"

Kiddo couldn't help but tap her on the nose when he saw a splotch of tomato paste on it. She didn't even flinch.

"He'd like anything you put on it," Kiddo answered. "But Sparks' one must have pineapple."

"You think she'd come?" Rue's face lit up. "She's always working."

"Or training others, or studying for her own self, or tinkering. But maybe if you do the asking, she'll take a break," Kiddo suggested.

Rue plonked the knife down immediately and dusted her hands.

"I'll find as many original Razes as I can," she said wholeheartedly, as if it had been her dream to collect them all... just to feed them pizza.

"I'll tell them to come and have an early dinner, and to see what I –" she paused, realising she was being uncharitable. "What *we* made."

"I did enjoy working as a team," Kiddo affirmed. He grabbed some mitts and pulled a specific tray from the oven, sliding the fresh pizza into a carboard take-out box. "Could you take this one as a delivery to the head doctors of the medical clinic?"

Rue peered over the top of the box as he quickly rolled the cutter over the pizza base.

"It's mostly vegetables. And not the good ones," Rue cringed. "Don't you like your doctors much?"

Narkon couldn't help but chuckle as he eavesdropped from the next work station.

"Actually, they'll be very happy if you assure them that every single ingredient is halal," Kiddo replied. "They will appreciate that."

"What the heck is that supposed to mean?" Rue took hold of the box as he placed it on her outstretched arms. "The ingredients are off?"

"Daleeah can explain it really well," Kiddo said. "It's about not using products with ingredients that might have hurt animals."

"In some faiths, there are products that are haram," Narkon tried to help.

Rue raised her eyebrows. "Ok. I'll tell them it's not a harem pizza."

Kiddo gaped.

"I'm sure they will be just as interested to hear that," Narkon told her, as she headed for the swinging doors.

"Rue, watch the road when you're crossing," Kiddo called after her.

She blew a raspberry, and was gone.

He truly felt like a negligent father, letting her go off alone. And yet, at some point tonight she would vanish again to continue to fend for herself as she always had.

He had to accept that she would probably be sleeping in a den full of psychopaths, with a newly stolen kitchen knife in hand.

Who knew what was in those pockets that she guarded so closely?

"I noticed when I arrived this morning that you hadn't wasted any time getting surveillance set up out the back," Narkon remarked. "The cameras were being installed first thing."

Kiddo got some more pizzas with assorted toppings into the oven. "Once something's on my to-do list, I want it off," he answered. "Act on it, or forget it by accident."

"I can understand why you didn't want to forget that," Narkon granted.

The chef was packing up as he neared the end of his shift.

"You did well with your students today," Kiddo congratulated him then. "I think this could become something they look forward to every weekend."

"I did better with these students than my normal ones, you think?" Narkon commented sardonically.

Kiddo grinned. "I know which version of you I preferred

learning from. But, no, you've adjusted your approach to suit what each audience needs."

He left the chef to it, and let the other cooks take over the oven baby-sitting when he heard the bell at the door jingling.

Sparks crossed straight to the counter, leaning right over it to collect a kiss from him.

Quicklips entered with a much older Hellion under his arm.

Still on their way, Seethe and Hato were like strong barricades on either side of Dom as they crossed the road together, and Rue was skipping about ecstatically ahead of them.

"I already messaged Jingle and Pash to get their butts here for a family dinner too," Sparks informed him. "So it'll be a full house before the dinner rush even starts."

"All we need is our active Razes to come home, and we'd be complete," Kid answered wistfully.

"Ooooh, but could we tolerate that many of us together nowadays?" Sparks pondered. "Trix would bring Blossom. Flip, Start, Velvet and Tiny would bring the recruit graduates. And then our current recruits might feel left out. I might as well start inviting my own apprentices at that point, let alone all of Frazzle and Daleeah's staff."

"I guess I'll have to book out the whole diner when that happens for Fraz and Dalee's wedding in a few months," Kiddo reflected. "I'll need to remember to warn the customers."

"You're adding that to your internal to-do list, aren't you?" Sparks chuckled affectionately.

He pulled out the diner's diary. "You got me. I might as well do it right now."

When Rue bounced back in she didn't hesitate to flit around to Kiddo's side of the counter.

"Please, take a seat," Rue told Sparks proudly. "We'll be right out with your pineapple pizza."

"How did you know?" Sparks put on an impressed expression. She joined the other Razes as they pulled some of the free standing tables and chairs together.

Kiddo plated up and told Rue who each specific pizza suited, and she was the most enthusiastic delivery girl he'd ever worked with.

"Which one are you going to choose for your own dinner?" he asked at last, selecting a plate for himself.

"Hmmm," she pointed one out with a colourful array of hot meats and peppers.

"You like very spicy?" he asked. That one was a backup helping for the insatiable Quicklips.

"Sure," she said, as if affronted that he would question the strength of her tastebuds.

"Alright," he acquiesced. "Today is your day for giving things a go."

He slid it onto a plate for her and they took seats beside each other at the Raze table.

"Who knew I would like crazy seafood pizza?" Dom asked Kid and Rue in fascination. "When I didn't even know."

"I picked it because of the mini octopuses," Rue told him pragmatically. "I was sure you'd think their puffy heads and tiny legs were funny."

Dom was straight faced and earnest. "You were right."

The others were talking and gorging themselves, but

Kiddo noticed Rue's face drop when she took a bite of her own. Her shoulders slumped.

She'd made the wrong choice.

Wordlessly, Kiddo put some slices of his own pizza on her plate, and went on eating.

She glanced up at him, uncertain.

"They're yours."

"You've done so many big, new things today," Kiddo replied. "I have plenty. And you've earned it."

She sniffed, rubbing at her nose roughly.

Probably the spices.

| 23 |

Twenty Three

Kiddo alternated between working and enjoying so many members of his family being together.

They were loud and rough and heckled each other, while Rue just soaked up the glory of being in the presence of so many under-web stars.

"I'm going to sneak out and grab Miss Dorris' brooch," Dom told Kiddo when it neared her usual evening arrival time. "Show her I appreciate it."

"Jingle and I will walk you over," Pash blotted at her flawless lips. "You relax for a bit," she told Hato. "We'll get The Lair going."

Sparks went with them, mentioning air fresheners and gangsters needing supervision.

Kiddo dished out second helpings to those staying behind, and only stopped in his tracks for a moment, brought back to reality, when he spotted two badged uniforms walking in – the sun setting behind them in a fiery blaze.

But then he recognised Koa and the completely relaxed posture of her partner.

"Hey," Kiddo greeted Koa, and nodded at her colleague, who was longingly eyeing the diner full of pizzas. "You're welcome to put in an order," Kid offered.

The male officer sighed. "This is a quick visit."

Then the male officer's gaze was dragged up, and up, to Hato's face as the big man met them at the counter.

"Hato," Koa didn't seem displeased to have found him here. "My partner and I took a second glance over last night's scene," she said – her body angling toward his.

"Thank you," Hato uttered – deep and gravelly. "I appreciate it."

Was he swelling in size?

"This is Officer Jeperd," Koa introduced the man with her. "One of the keen cops I was telling you I work with."

"Great to meet you! We've all heard a lot about you," Jeperd extended a hand.

Kiddo swallowed a snort of laughter. Hato's bicep was nearly the size of this man's head, and Kiddo was certain he saw a slight flex there when Hato reached out to engulf that hand in return.

"Jeperd, I bet you only had time to help us because you're on break," Kiddo tried to give Hato a proper way in. "Come grab a coffee."

It wasn't hard to convince Jeperd that he deserved the caffeine hit, and he stepped away from Koa and Hato to take up a stool.

Kiddo slid the officer a plate of pizza to stretch the time a little further too.

It was only when Koa and Jeperd absolutely had to get

back to their patrol that Kiddo realised Rue must have been scared off by their presence.

Her spot was empty, and he couldn't help but be disheartened by the idea of her being alone again.

"Appreciate the distraction," Hato mumbled in an even lower voice than usual, almost conspiratorially. "I got her personal number so we can communicate directly."

"Sounds romantic," Kiddo teased.

Hato remained deadpan. "She said there were some possible scrape marks out there. It could be from someone getting dragged, or it could be from your cooks heaving heavy bins across the ground. But there were no other clear clues to read."

Kiddo grunted in frustration.

"Was that your kid who fled when the law got here?" the Hellion with Quicklips asked Kiddo in a smoky voice.

Maybe all Hellions were similar to Madam Hellion. It might have been a requirement to sound tough and weathered. Many of them had the same long, white hair that their Madam sported too.

"You let her go out unsupervised?" the woman husked.

Kiddo sensed some distinct judgment there.

"She's not one of ours," Seethe drawled. "She's a baby snatcher."

"She's not a snatcher," Kiddo defended. "Yet. And I'm hoping we can help her to keep it that way."

"Yorak is using the kid to spy on you," Quicklips said uncomfortably.

"Yes, but, I think we can win her over," Kiddo answered resolutely. "We can offer her more than he can."

"He can offer the brat her life," Seethe picked at his teeth.

"And we can offer her a *happy* life," Kiddo stacked a pile of dirty plates for the wait staff to collect.

"You've barely known her a week," Seethe argued lazily. "Who knows how deep the Wolf has his claws in her."

That was precisely the kind of thing Kiddo wanted to get Rue away from.

"You took me in as soon as you found me, and I was way more of a hassle than she could be," Kid said.

Seethe wore an evil smirk, but he spoke plaintively. "Maybe we learned our lesson."

"Hey, it could work out," Quicklips supported Kiddo. "I mean, look at *you*," he said to Seethe. "By all accounts, you used to be the worst. Now you're practically a saint."

"Yes, well I've clearly seen the light of doing good." Seethe inspected his purple knuckles, which were always bruised from smacking around too many snatchers.

"She needs a chance. That kid is the poster child for trauma and neglect," the Hellion grunted roughly, as if she were describing the misguided lead singer of a sad band.

"Yes. We've all been there," Quicklips declared. "We've all got our tough, or hard working, or larrikin armour on, after years of working ourselves out. She's probably just trying to get there with her own little set of armour too."

The Hellion reached up to lightly pinch his cheek, as if he was just the darndest thing himself for being so empathetic.

"Hey Kid." One of the waitresses approached Kiddo then. "Miss Dorris' china teacup has a chip in it. Do we have a spare?"

Kiddo nodded absently. "I'll sort it." He opened a cupboard under the counter that stored delicate items separately.

He'd been so preoccupied, he hadn't noticed Miss Dorris coming in.

"Good evening, Miss Dorris," Kid approached her with a new, steaming cup. "Do you feel better after seeing Raze tonight?"

She beamed at him. "Thank you dear, I'll look forward to it."

Kiddo paused. "You don't recall seeing him yet?"

Dom usually would have hung about to spend time with Miss Dorris. He would actually be sitting in the booth with her right now if he'd come back already.

"I don't think so," the old lady answered placidly. She pulled her new teacup closer, admiring its flowers and butter-flies.

Kiddo was already shoving past the other Razes, who were now getting ready to head off for their Saturday night patrols.

"Kid?" Quicklips called after him.

Kiddo dashed about the front carpark, then sprinted to the back.

Nerves racing, he bolted for the warehouse.

"Would you be *careful?*" Seethe yanked him to a stop by the back of his shirt. "Any time you feel the need to run off, consider that you could be going into an ambush."

Kiddo shoved at him and broke back into a run for the warehouse.

"Sparks," he skidded to a stop too late, half colliding with the Bullet boss, Sora's back.

"Sparks ..." he panted again as she appeared from where she'd been hidden by Sora's size. "... Did Dom stay here with you?"

Apprehension touched her face. "He only came in for a couple of minutes to find something. He headed back to the diner a while ago."

"Ah, shit," Seethe cussed behind Kid.

Kiddo reeled around. "You're going to get straight to your patrol," he told Quicklips as the others caught up. "You and Hato take the bikes to do a search through the streets. Seethe and I will leg it around the immediate area."

"We won't bring the recruits into it yet," Hato decided. "I'll tell Jeffrey he can take a turn leading general check-ins tonight." He jabbed a finger at Sora, who'd overheard everything. "You keep your mouth shut."

The Silver Bullet nodded curtly.

Jeffrey yowled like a cowboy winning rodeo when he got his orders, and Quicklips and Hato revved their bikes to life.

Kiddo and Seethe didn't wait around – jogging doggedly through the well-lit areas, and then scouring the same dark kinds of places that Rue had been attacked in by the teen snatchers.

Sparks had sent out a group message to ask if Dom had turned up with the other Razes, and Kiddo kept glancing at his phone anxiously.

Pash: he's not in The Lair, doll ...

Jingle: I've checked everywhere I can think on the base. Kid's new cameras show he didn't return to the diner, but they only cover the back and some of the front carpark.

Frazzle: not at clinic.

Tiny: I messaged him today. He said he was doing fine!

"Let's circle back," Seethe said raggedly. "See if we missed something."

Jingle: a fire escape sensor just went off ...

Kid: we're close. We'll check it. Stay put.

Kiddo and Seethe picked up the pace, rounding the block and hurrying back to base. They took the stairs two at a time.

Lungs bursting and legs burning, they threw themselves up onto the rooftop.

And found Dom, sitting near the ledge, gazing out at the streets below.

| 24 |

Twenty Four

Seethe caught at Kiddo before he raced forward, as if worried they might alarm Dom.

They were both surprised to see him upright.

It had been unspoken, but both of them had been grimly scanning for an unconscious shape in the bushes. Or even a murder victim.

Seethe sent a quick message to say they'd got him, as Kiddo cautiously stepped closer to the ledge.

"Dom?" Kiddo asked.

Dom peered over his shoulder.

"Kid," he said slowly, as if processing who he was seeing.

His lips were purple. He looked frozen.

He hadn't thought to grab his leather jacket before dinner.

"Where'd you get to when you left the diner?" Seethe asked, approaching unhurriedly from Dom's other side.

Dom started, as if he'd only just noticed Seethe was there. Then he shivered with the cold.

"I just wandered for a long while," Dom shrugged. "I forgot what I was meant to be doing so I had to think about it."

"You did what you'd intended to do already," Kiddo reassured him. "You came to find this."

Dom's gaze followed Kid's hand as it touched the sparkly peacock brooch that had been pinned to Dom's t-shirt, over his heart. Dom himself must have pinned it there to keep from losing it.

"I did?" Dom asked in consternation. "Why would I want that?"

He touched his head then; jumbled.

"No, I wouldn't forget Miss Dorris. I remember now."

Kiddo rubbed Dom's chilled hands in his.

"I have no idea why I'm up here," Dom sighed. "Maybe I just wanted to come home without upsetting anyone on the ground floor."

"It's good you found your way back," Seethe answered. "Really good."

The last time Seethe had lost Dom, it had taken Dom ten years to find his way back.

"I want to go inside," Dom told them. "My head is killing me. And I'm really cold."

"Alright, we'll get you to bed," Kiddo vowed.

Without rushing, Kid helped Dom up. He was unsteady, but he seemed to be surfacing to greater clarity as they moved.

This time Frazzle came to the bedroom to check Dom over again.

"More blood noses? Feel sick?" the doctor asked, while peering into Dom's eyes. "Any new signs of a fall?"

"Just the dizzy headache," Dom grumbled, squinting. "And being a human block of ice."

"There's an hour or so he can't account for," Kiddo also chipped in. He sat on the bed beside Dom, his arm around Dom's back.

"Hmm," Frazzle nodded slowly. "One too many falls and head jolts is not good. Can have serious effects."

"What did Daleeah and your colleagues say about the first scans?" Kiddo asked. "You wanted to check some things."

"Is interesting," Frazzle answered carefully.

Seethe's eyes were sharp. "What does 'interesting' mean, doc?"

Frazzle rubbed his chin. "Almost looked like signs of head shocking, as much as knock to the head."

"Shocking?" Kiddo repeated. "As in, *electric* shock?"

"Oh my lord," Dom groaned. "Did I put a knife in a toaster? Or play with Pash's hairdryer in the bath … and then just dawdle off to the diner yesterday? What is wrong with me?"

"No, no," Frazzle patted his arm. "Would be a shock straight into cranium. But more likely trauma from head knocks that don't get chances to recover. Symptoms should settle, we scan again soon to check is reversing. In meantime, we keep close watch on you for recovery."

"Great," Dom intoned, still shuddering with the cold.

"We won't let him out of our sight," Seethe asserted darkly.

"I bet you will," Dom returned. "Seeing as I plan to have a nice, hot shower as soon as the doctor leaves."

"*Kiddo* won't let him out of his sight," Seethe corrected.

And Dom stopped any show of bravado when Kiddo closed the bathroom door.

While Kiddo got the water running, Dom fumbled to un-clip Miss Dorris' brooch and to put it safely aside. He let Kiddo draw his thin t-shirt up, over his head, and then he gingerly kicked off his shoes and pants.

When they stood together under the stream of water, Dom circled his arms around Kiddo's neck and leaned his forehead on Kid's shoulder.

Heating up and silently processing.

Kiddo ran his fingers up and down Dom's spine and inky skin, just letting him be.

He traced rippled feeling burn marks, trailed over shoulder muscles, and stroked Dom's dripping hair backward – careful to avoid where the sore, bruised spot on his scalp seemed to be.

"Kid," Dom said eventually, turning his face toward Kiddo's neck. "I *really* love you."

He drew in a big ragged breath.

"My dream self and my awake self truly believes that I'm safe with you. You love me. You are always helping me."

Kiddo paused his movements and pressed his arms around Dom tightly. "I love you, too. And I won't let you forget it."

| 25 |

Twenty Five

Dom fretted his way through more terrible nightmares all night.

Then Kiddo had a hard time keeping Dom from wresting the recruits from Quicklips and Seethe the next morning. He wanted to go back to feeling like a normal Raze, and the recruits' loud support didn't help.

Seethe was just threatening to smack Dom unconscious again so that he'd stay still, and to do the same to any sooking recruits, when Rue showed her face.

"I wonder who would win in a fight between you two," Rue commented, startling them all.

"Me," Dom and Seethe answered at the same time.

"Why would you want to hit Raze?" Rue asked Seethe then. "You love him."

Seethe crossed his arms. "Love's a strong word. Especially when he's being annoying."

"Dom got confused again last night," Kiddo told her. "He needs to rest his brain. You should help me to keep him from misbehaving."

Rue paled and ducked her head, as if truly bothered by the news that Dom had had another memory blank. She shoved her fists in her pockets.

"I keep wandering off," Dom sighed at her melodramatically. "I'm going to need one of those baby leashes soon."

But Kiddo was relieved to watch Dom climb up and lay back against the windshield of Sparks' Jeep.

He was throwing in the gauntlet.

"Does your brain still work well enough to read what this says?" Rue tested him. "Don't give it away," she warned Kiddo and Seethe.

She gradually traced a word on the bonnet, like they'd done yesterday. She paused as she got stuck on the first letter for a moment, writing the 's' backwards, then rubbing it off to re-do it properly.

"Hmmm," Dom pondered, considering her squiggly markings gravely. "Have you been spending time with Pash?"

She rolled her eyes. "Just have a go if you aren't sure. Don't avoid it."

There went another piece of Kiddo's heart, floating off to land in her hands without her realising it.

A tiny smile quirked in the corner of Dom's lips as he nodded and concentrated. "I know this one. It's why I thought Pash had got at you. It says 'sale,' doesn't it?"

Rue was the one who lifted her palm, and Dom was deeply gratified to be awarded a high five.

Even Seethe appeared momentarily touched, but he quickly reassembled his usual, lethal expression and turned on his heel to join Quicklips. Probably afraid he was going soft.

"It said that word on a sign at a bookshop I pass all the time," she told him. "I've been doing what you said – sounding out words in my head everywhere, and I'm already getting faster," she finished smugly.

Dom was beyond delighted, and hardly noticed the day passing after Kiddo brought them a notepad to fill up with words and sentences.

They paid no heed to the general noise of any gangsters still living in the space, blocked out the random shouts and thuds of training recruits, ignored the revving of engines, and automatically snacked off whatever plates of food Kiddo put in front of them.

The next day Rue was back, and this time they sat at the dining table, coming up with a story about Duncan Jr. while Kiddo did paperwork and tried not to eavesdrop.

Rue came up with the crazy adventures that their fish apparently got involved in at night, and Dom helped her to slowly eke the letters out.

The following day one of the new housekeepers that Jingle had hired presented the two of them with a pack of crayons, so of course they had to illustrate the story.

Sparks and Kiddo applauded when Rue read the finished product out to them, and Sparks was misty-eyed at how much this tough child's face glowed when Dom whispered clues to help her along.

"I'm going to have to keep a closer eye on that fish," Kiddo decided.

He nearly felt his heart stop when Rue slipped her hand into Dom's, tugging at him to walk her downstairs so she could leave them again.

Even Rue seemed to become despondent when she decided it was time to say goodbye of an evening.

"Is that book sale still on at the shop you pass by?" Dom asked her, when another of her visits wrapped up at the end of the week.

"Think so, why?"

Dom slipped a note from his pocket and gave it to her.

She stared at the cash.

"I have more scans tomorrow," Dom told her forlornly, starting to descend. "You should buy your favourite book and bring it over to cheer me up. I'll pick a good one from our library too, and we can compare."

There was much more money there than what one book from a discount sale would cost.

"Alright," she accepted that excitedly. "I'll go shopping for the best cover, but I'll also check what it says on the back," she promised.

It was only at the end of Rue's visits each night, when he'd walked her out and the magic was over, that Dom noticed his head aching or getting dizzy again. He was adamant that *she* was the one who seemed to be getting increasingly upset at their goodbyes outside the warehouse. But he always walked her to the corner, until she wouldn't let him escort her any further, because he hated letting her go too.

Dom was always left tired out when she left, and headed to bed to let his head throb through more nightmares.

Nevertheless, each day Rue made all the difference, and Kiddo hoped so much rest was helping Dom's brain to slowly recover.

On the morning of Dom's appointment, Kiddo was hardly surprised when Rue plonked herself down in the waiting room chair at Kiddo's side.

She acted as if it was totally natural for her to meet there unannounced to keep Kid company.

He stopped twisting his ring in anxious circles, glad to see her.

She held a small hardcover book with a sunny yellow jacket.

"Hey, tomorrow's Saturday," she announced. "Should we go to your chef's class together again?"

"Sounds good," he agreed casually. "Narkon was planning on doing a dessert day tomorrow. We could make a cake."

"Ooooh," she gushed, hugging the book to her stomach as if she was visualising the scrumptiousness already. "I still haven't decided when I want my birthday to be, so that you guys can have a party. I could make it be tomorrow, seeing as there'll be a cake."

Kiddo considered for a moment. "Well, it's an important choice. It might be a better idea to pick carefully, and simply enjoy the cake tomorrow for the sake of it."

"Can't I just change my birthday next year if I want a different day?" she frowned.

"You could," Kiddo admitted. "But, I remembered you saying you wanted to grow up to be clever and to have a good job. And a birthday might be key to that."

She snorted. "What's that got to do with birthdays and cakes?" she started letting the book flap open and closed in her hands, the pages fanning out and then snapping shut.

"You might decide that you're ready to go to school soon,

to help you prepare for your future," Kiddo explained. "And for that, we'll need to get you a birth certificate."

"I'm meant to get a certificate for being born?" she spluttered incredulously. "There were no awards for having me! Rue the day, remember?"

"You might not have been given an official identity," Kiddo admitted. "Which makes it hard to live outside the snatcher world. But Jingle could help you to get a certificate with a birthday for identification, like a pass to the real world."

She contemplated that. She swung her legs and set the book in her lap.

"I don't think school would suit me, even if I have a certificate and a birthday."

Kiddo grimaced. "At least you're starting out well, with a goal. But I admit, school definitely didn't suit me. I had to work very hard to get through it so that I could meet my own goals."

"Now you have a diner," she mused, impressed.

"You'll have to put up with rules and feeling pretty different to the other kids," Kiddo told her. "And you might get frustrated or have blow-ups every now and then. But, if I can get through it, anyone can."

"You had Hato to keep you on track," Rue reflected a little down heartedly. "Didn't you?"

It had taken Hato, Flip, Seethe, Tiny and Jingle to help Kiddo start to resemble anything close to human. Hato and Seethe had been about Kiddo's age now, when they'd taken Kid on as a thirteen year old disaster.

"Yes. And you'll have Dom and I."

Rue seemed to become even more downcast, slipping her hands into her pockets.

Dom's laughter could be heard from the corridor then, before he chortled his way into the waiting room.

Daleeah followed him, wearing a feigned cross expression.

"What's so funny?" Rue asked, still seeming somewhat sensitive.

"What did he do?" Kiddo asked, more poignantly.

Daleeah gave Dom a dry look. "I asked him how his memory seems today."

"And I told her that I remember her wedding was superb," Dom announced. But then he straightened, "which of course, it will be."

Rue groaned. "You're being silly. This lady is a doctor, don't waste her time."

"Here is somebody with appropriate respect," Daleeah announced. "And with wonderful non-'harem' pizza delivery skills."

The doctor quirked an eyebrow at Kiddo.

So Rue really had gone off last weekend and reassured the clinicians they weren't eating concubine pizza.

"Tomorrow your delivery might be cake," Rue informed Dalee. "Kiddo and I were just talking about it. But not birthday cake specifically."

Dom smartened right up. "Cake, huh? I'm hungry right now. Why don't we head to Kid's Place for a bite?"

Daleeah waved them off. "We'll tell you when the scans have been reviewed. Go and enjoy."

"You know …" this time Rue paused considerately before Kiddo had to tell her to check the road. Her energy was slowly returning. "Your doctors have never been mentioned as being Razes for sale."

"That's a relief," Kiddo replied, nodding for her to go ahead and cross.

"I wonder why?" she questioned. "They've got such valuable skills."

"Luckily, they might be seen more as helping the Raze gang from the sidelines," Dom surmised. "Rather than being part of the action and gaining worth for rebelliousness."

"And too many normal people would notice if anything happened to Dalee," Kid added. "She came from the real world."

Kiddo opened the door for them, and noticed Narkon at the counter with Teddy.

"What am I doing here?" Narkon interjected before he could ask.

Kiddo closed his mouth.

"He's collecting his payment before his university classes start," Teddy supplied.

There was a morning coffee and a plate of bacon and scrambled eggs in front of the chef.

Kiddo raised his eyebrows. "Glad you have been taking payment. I was becoming suspicious of all those charity hours."

"Hi chef," Rue acknowledged Narkon as she slid into a booth after Dom. "Can't wait for cake tomorrow..."

"I'm looking forward to our weekend session again myself," Narkon stated pleasantly.

"Let's hope I don't wander off and lose my marbles again this time," Dom said with distaste.

Rue shoved him, suddenly sulky and grumpy again at the idea of it.

"Have you been … well?" Narkon asked delicately.

Teddy and most others were not aware of exactly what had benched Raze recently.

"Dandy," Dom lied. "Rue has been taking care of me."

"That's so nice," Teddy approved. "I thought you were meant to be Raze's enemy," she said to Rue. "This is much better."

Rue's face turned bright red, and her head sank down on her shoulders as if she was a turtle getting ready to withdraw into her shell.

"Rue would never hurt me," Dom said lightly, though with sympathy in his eyes as he recognised her discomfort.

It had seemed lately that Rue had been letting go of the snatcher she was expected to be becoming. But she'd just been unavoidably reminded that they actually weren't meant to be friends.

Suddenly lashing out, she threw the yellow book she'd carried over with her into Dom's face. "That's my *job*, idiot," she half sobbed.

She buried her head in her arms on the table.

Rubbing his cheek where the sharp corner of the book had hit, Dom bent toward her tentatively.

"Sorry Rue," he said gently. "The weird lines between us get blurry. But snatcher stuff is obviously a trigger, and we don't need to talk about it."

She was making some very wet sounds from her cocoon on the tabletop.

Dom lifted a tangled lock of her feathery red hair to try to see her face.

"It's alright, Rue. You're learning every day, and Kiddo and I are learning about you too," Dom went on.

Rue's body was shaking, but she shot an arm out and hit Dom in the chest so that he knew to stay back.

Dom gave them all a helpless gaze, at a loss.

Teddy shuffled closer to their table. "I'm sorry I made you sad," she said tenderly. "Did you need a big hug?"

There was more juicy snuffling. After a moment, Rue's head moved up and down.

"There, there," Teddy cooed. She reached for Rue.

And though Teddy was a short person herself, the size of her heart and its power to care gave her the strength of a weightlifter. She hauled Roo up into her arms, and didn't even totter when Roo surprisingly wrapped herself around Teddy like a koala.

They caught a glimpse of how flustered and overheated Rue's face had become, seeming to radiate with emotion, before she buried it into Teddy's hair. She howled while Teddy swayed her to and fro.

"Let's go splash our faces," Teddy suggested, carrying Rue towards the bathrooms like the baby she always protested against being called.

Dom winced, picking the book up from where it had landed open on its back.

"It's called 'My Big Family'," Dom read the title dejectedly. "This poor kid wants us. But she's conflicted."

"She has a big, bad Wolf haunting her," Kiddo agreed.

"Telling her we are the enemy. It would be terrifying, and confusing."

Narkon had gone and Kiddo was plating up some pancakes by the time Teddy re-emerged with Rue in tow.

Rue's hair had been smoothed and wetted to cool her down, and her face was no longer grubby. But the skin of her cheeks was still blotchily red, and she couldn't lift her head as she sidled heavily into the spot next to Dom again.

Kiddo silently thanked Teddy before he set the three plates of pancakes on the table and sat opposite Dom and Rue.

"You knew exactly how I would like my pancakes," Dom complimented Kiddo with a steady, upbeat tone. "Half syrup and half strawberry jam." He rolled up a big flap of pancake, making it into a scroll, and conquered it in a bite.

Kiddo's had a sparing dash of butter, while he'd opted to put scoops of ice-cream on Rue's plate.

She sniffed, head still bowed, and took up her spoon. She sullenly worked through a ball of melting vanilla.

"I know how much you struggle to pick between sugary flavours," Kiddo carried on the conversation with Dom. "So I thought I'd give you both, after being so brave at your appointment."

"I'm glad to have had the two of you with me," Dom said around a mouthful. "I never had good experiences with clinics when I was young, so it could have been tough going there. Except I knew I had you waiting."

Kiddo just needed Sparks beside him and everything would be complete.

Rue tried to take one big breath that juddered into three

gulped breaths instead, as she wiped ice-cream from her chin with the back of her hand.

"I'm sorry I hurt you ... with the book," she said haltingly, with eyes lowered.

She pushed her plate away.

"I'm sorry I was light-hearted about whether snatchers and Razes might hurt each other," Dom told her. "Sometimes jokes help me to deal with things."

She moved a bit closer to him. "Better than hurting someone you like ... by hitting them with a book."

Dom moved the storybook across the table so that it was within her reach, and traced the title with a lotus tattooed finger.

"Did you still want to read this one together?" he asked.

She shook her head quickly. "The title made me happy when I read it out in the shop." Her eyes reddened again. "But it's upsetting me now."

She still hadn't recovered.

"That's ok," he replied. "We'll read it together another time."

"You could add it to our library," Kiddo suggested. "Then it'll be safe, and you can come back and read it with us when you're up to it."

She was quiet for a few moments, before she nodded.

"How about you take Dom to the library now?" Kiddo suggested. "By the time I clean this up, you'll have found a place for your book, and picked one for Dom to read to you."

Dom tucked 'My Big Family' into his jacket pocket, and shooed her out ahead of himself. "We'll be waiting for you," Dom told Kiddo.

And he followed Rue's sad little form from the diner.

| 26 |

Twenty Six

"What happened?"

Kiddo was shocked to find Jingle and Pash hovering over Dom on the library floor.

'My Big Family' had fallen from his hand, and a number of other books had been knocked from a shelf by the arched window.

"No clue," Dom held his head in his hands.

Jingle rose, her hand on her heart as if she'd suffered a terrible fright.

"Your snatcher baby screamed so shrilly I heard her from my room," Jingle grimaced. "Dom must have had a dizzy spell and scared the life out of the kid when he collapsed."

Dom gave a drawn out groan. "Poor thing. She was already in a state, wasn't she?" he asked in consternation. "And I freaked her right out."

Pash was bemused. "I tried to tell her that Dom probably just did too much today, but the kid was having none of it. She was hysterical. And then she was feral. There was no stopping her getting out of here in her panic."

Kiddo crouched down in front of Dom. "There might have been too much excitement for the *both* of you today."

"I'm starting to recall some pancakes, hissy fits. A book to the face." Dom blinked at the upturned cover. "This is an awful way to make her feel like we could be her new stable, 'big family'."

"It's not like you're doing it on purpose, honey," Pash tsked. He took Dom's forearm and got him standing. "You didn't even know who *we* were when we first burst in here."

Kiddo shared a glance with Jingle at those words, and she gave a short, upset nod.

"Well, it's all come back to me now," Dom said. "No need to fuss. I know you're Jangle, you're Posh and this hot one must be ..."

"The love of your life," Kiddo asserted flatly.

"Mmm. Sparkles, is it?"

Kiddo put the fallen books back onto the shelf, making sure the bright yellow jacket of Rue's was easy to spot.

"I don't care if you're tired or not," Kiddo lectured. "You're –"

"Definitely going to bed," Dom finished. "I'm wiped."

The lack of argument was unexpected, but Kiddo was relieved to tuck Dom in firmly, and laid beside him on the bed.

They were quiet, lost in thought, until the bedroom door opened and closed, and Dom patted the other side of the mattress for Sparks to join them.

Dom reached to tuck her hair behind her ear.

"Nice earrings," he said simply, trying to ignore the concern in her expression. He touched the closest gold tipped stud. "Are they your lucky stars?"

"No, silly," she nestled down against him. "You and Kiddo are my two lucky stars."

Dom and Kiddo smiled at each other. Neither of them had realised that. And yet she was always saying she was thankful for them – thanking her lucky stars on a daily basis.

"Did you really forget Jingle and Pash?" Sparks asked softly then.

She didn't go further to ask if he had forgotten anyone else.

Dom watched as Kiddo listlessly began to test his ring on each of Dom's fingers, twirling it and slipping it from digit to digit.

"Only for a bit," Dom said. "I think I forget who *I* even am when I drop out like that. I just never see it coming."

It would have petrified Rue when it had happened.

"We'll see what Frazzle and Daleeah have to say about how far you've come since the first scans," Kiddo stated. "They'll have some ideas."

"At worst, you'll spend another week drafting up adventures for Duncan Jr. with Rue," Sparks said with false certainty. "And at best, you'll be playing pranks on Jeffrey and the others by morning."

"That's my 'at best' scenario?" Dom smirked. "Really?"

"What would you prefer?" Sparks queried. "Enlighten us, and we might be able to make it happen."

Dom shuffled a little, settling in. "Alright," he said thoughtfully. "In my best case scenario," he mulled it over, with a serene smile tugging at his lips. "I am waking up to a bed with the three of us in it."

"That's easy," Sparks granted, gesturing a hand at their current set up.

"Our mechanic-ess has taken a holiday, so she doesn't have to rush off to study, to teach, to experiment or to fix anything. Kiddo has also shown Rue the fastest routes to run to school when she's late, so Kiddo can stay in bed too."

"Oh, we have a daughter," Sparks breathed.

"Teaching her to run instead of to be organised? Does that sound like a responsible solution?" Kiddo asked. "Though I guess Hato did the same with me. I didn't leave him much choice."

"Oh yes," Dom went on. "The irresponsible thing is that we all had to stay up late to help her with her lessons. She has so much catching up to do."

"Between us, we can do it," Sparks decided.

"And it's only fair that, whenever she's in trouble and struggling to adjust, Kiddo goes in to face the principal," Dom yawned.

"How is that fair?" Kid grouched.

Sparks shot him an 'are you joking?' expression.

"Alright, I guess I did the same to Hato. But, maybe we could make Grandfather Hato go in for Rue as well, seeing as he has all the experience."

Dom chortled.

"So, in your best case scenario, we are presuming Rue would like us for her family, and Hato is going to do the frightening adult stuff. Aside from that, you just want us all waking up together?" Sparks took them back to the start of the story.

"Oh, and when we wake up, you and Kiddo are wearing nothing," Dom added for good measure.

"Which means you are also wearing nothing," Kiddo insisted.

"Because even though we all stayed up late helping Rue, we three stayed up even later together after that," Dom said with satisfaction.

"Nice," Sparks remarked. "I bet we enjoyed that."

"Oh, we did," Dom avowed. "I especially enjoyed watching Kiddo kiss his way along your spine ..."

"Love when he does that," Sparks bit her lip.

"... And when I got to flip you over and kiss up along your legs," Dom continued. "While of course Kiddo held you, touched you, and kissed your neck."

"This best case scenario is going well," Kiddo commented. "We're very smooth."

"I love that Kiddo hits you with the rough and tumble stuff," Sparks told Dom. "And then mourns over any rips to your buttons and shirts."

Kiddo sighed sorrowfully.

"*Thennnnn,* in this scenario, we go about our day, being the best Razes we can be," Dom went on. "We are surrounded in our other Razes. We help Rue. And we do the rest all again at night too."

"It sounds achievable," Kiddo reflected.

"It sounds lovely," Sparks attested.

"We'll work on making it happen," Dom finished.

He steepled his fingertip against Kiddo's so that the ring cascaded back down onto the finger of its rightful owner.

"I'm so lucky," he said, with a furrowed brow. "I'm safe with you. You love me. You are always helping me."

Then Dom took first Kiddo's hand, brushing a feather light kiss along Kiddo's knuckles, before next taking Spark's hand. He turned it to delicately kiss the sensitive skin along the inside of her wrist.

He relaxed then, his eyes on Sparks and his spine pressed to Kiddo's body. She stroked his forehead and along his nose until those blue eyes eventually closed.

When Dom had fallen into a fitful sleep, Sparks gave kisses to both of her lucky stars before she withdrew, and Kiddo stayed by the bedside.

Dom repeated his reassuring phrases as he dreamed, often muttering the last words he'd said as though they were comforting him. And Kiddo hoped they truly were helping him to stave off the nightmares that had become so regular lately.

"I'm safe with you. You love me. You are always helping me."

While he watched over Dom, Kid organised Narkon to manage the night shift and asked one of the waitresses to get Miss Dorris home safely if she came in. Then he pottered around the room, quietly neatening things. He folded Dom's leather jacket, and placed Miss Dorris' brooch into a nice box in the bedside drawers for safe keeping.

He only considered letting Dom be when Jingle messaged the group chat, asking for a family meeting before everyone had to do their evening duties.

He cast an eye around the room.

The window was locked from the inside, Dom was tucked in, and Kid would be just one level below.

"You're safe with me. You love me – just as I love you. I am always here to help you," Kiddo whispered the lulling words to Dom. And then he closed the door inaudibly.

He met the others on the living level, surprised to find Jingle gathering everyone onto the couches rather than at the dining table.

She had the TV set up with the group chat open, ready to share the screen. Trix, Blossom and even Ryo were on one half of the large screen, while Flip, Velvet, Tiny and Start were on the other. They appeared to be congregated in a hotel room, sharing a device together.

The glow of the TV in the unlit room made the edges of Jingle's face seem sharper, highlighting how nervous she appeared.

"What's going on Jingle?" Hato asked solemnly.

She wrung her hands as she turned to address them.

"I received a parcel delivery just before," she said, swallowing. "It had a virtu-disc in it, and a note from the Wolf."

"What did the note say?" Flip asked with a darkening expression, his voice crackling over the connection.

Jingle cleared her throat uneasily. "It said 'for family movie night'."

"Yorak might have wanted us all to gather in one place..." Pash said in warning, becoming tense at once.

Jingle nodded. "I know. I asked Quicklips to make sure the recruits keep close on patrols around the warehouse. Jeffrey is going to open The Lair." She wrapped her arms around herself in a hug. "But I really didn't want to watch it first alone."

"Of course not," Sparks jumped in soothingly. "Yorak actually got it right. We should face things as a family."

"Any idea what's on the disc?" Trix questioned. She was seated on Blossom's lap, but her face was deadly serious.

"No," Jingle cringed. "All I did was check it for viruses and spyware, and it was clear of all that."

Seethe leaned forward. His elbows on his knees. "Only one way to find out what's on it then."

Jingle nodded apprehensively, opening screen share mode so that the overseas Razes shrank down to a corner.

She was just pressing play on the unnamed file, at the same time that Frazzle hurried up the stairs.

"No symptoms reversal!" Frazzle puffed urgently, as if he'd run all the way. "White matter injury ... is like Raze is the receiver of ... ongoing shock trauma..."

He petered off as the sounds of a scuffle came from the TV.

Blurs of coloured lights and a sign suggested the scuffle was moving from the front car park of Kid's Place to the back. Someone was being very quickly dragged.

The jolting camera-work finally stilled, with whoever wore the bodycam stepping back from the melee. A pile of snatchers were furiously trying to subdue someone who was almost totally smothered by their bodies.

"Calm down, Raze," the Wolf's pleasant voice spoke from beside the Hunter in the bodycam. "You're scaring the little one."

The Wolf seemed to pass someone small over to the

bodycam Hunter then, and there was just enough light to see fluffy red hair coming into view at the bottom of the lens.

The speakers on the TV were filled with Rue's breaths, which were punctuated by gulping sobs as she hyperventilated and hiccupped.

"*Please* take it easy Raze," Yorak said pacifyingly. "The little one made sure to let me know you'd be out here alone. I would hate to follow through on my threat to snap her neck if we don't succeed with you for tonight's round."

The camera shifted sightly as the Hunter's arms tightened around the child, gagging her mouth to try to stifle her crying.

Rue let out one more wail, but it was muffled now.

And the struggle beneath the pile of snatchers stopped.

"Yes," Yorak went on. "I knew my Raze would understand how easy it would be to break such a small neck as this one. And tonight is so important in stepping things up, that I really need your co-operation."

Facing less resistance, the snatchers hurried to rearrange themselves – taking tight holds on their captive's limbs, forcing his wrists behind his back, pressing their knees into his shoulders and forcing his cheek down against the gravel. It was as if he were the most ferocious criminal, being arrested by the law.

"What … do you want?" Dom's voice uttered venomously from the ground.

"You and Kiddo," Yorak reminded him. "And I'm happy to work for it."

"You'll … never … be able to … work hard enough … for that."

Dom suddenly bucked, and managed to head butt the snatcher who had been gripping his face, making the snatcher reel back for a moment.

There was fondness in Yorak's voice. "Hard to get, is not impossible to get. Especially after Raff was so helpful, chipping away at your armour before his work was cut short." Now the voice grew speculative. "You've forced me to ramp things up and act faster than I would like here. But I need to seal the deal while you're weak enough to be susceptible to suggestion."

Rue squeaked and the camera wobbled as the Hunter apparently gave her a squeeze for Dom to hear.

"And there are incentives for you in all of this," Yorak added calmly.

Dom stilled again at the fearful sounds from Rue.

"For instance, if you stop doing yourself damage by struggling, and let *me* hurt you just a little bit more, I will make sure the child leaves here safely. If she continues to keep her mouth shut, she will be fine."

Yorak stepped closer to Dom, kneeling down beside him and appearing in the camera's gaze for the first time.

The Wolf gestured to someone, and a phone torch lit up.

"Hmm. I can see the fight still in your eyes," Yorak said with dissatisfaction. "If you don't relax, it won't work."

"Would *you* be relaxed?" Dom hissed.

The Wolf conceded to that. "Granted, this will actually

hurt much more than 'just a little bit'. Much more than other times. But for her sake, you must try."

Rue's cries were muffled, but constant.

"It might be nice for you to hear that the little wretch started to care for you long before you saw and could remember her," the Wolf went on. "She tried not to," he chuckled. "Even called you an idiot when you could hardly get back on your bike after our encounters, or nearly got yourself hit by a car in your blank state. But do you now vaguely remember her taking your hand, and guiding you until you started to become aware each time?"

Even though it was faint, Rue sounded heartbroken. Fast becoming hysterical.

"She never knew I was aware of what a tool she was becoming. But here we are, and this time she's counting on you."

Yorak was still watching Dom's eyes, and now he seemed content with what he saw.

"What do you say?" Yorak asked. "Fight me? Or let me in, take the pain, and allow the child to live?"

"So let … the kid go then," Dom bit out.

The Hunter at once unwrapped his tight hold around Rue, and shoved the wailing child away so hard that she skittered off to fall against the dumpsters.

"You see?" Yorak said. "Man of my word."

Then the Wolf pressed something similar to a stun gun to the side of Dom's head, freezing Dom entirely with a blast of sharp, flickering currents.

Yorak waited an agonising five seconds, before shutting off the stream. Then he gestured for the snatchers to fall back.

Yorak pulled Dom into a sitting position in front of himself, bracing Dom's floppy body with his hands.

He leaned in beside Dom's ear and whispered something until Dom started to rouse.

Then the Wolf pulled back, and took hold of Dom's chin, almost pressing their foreheads together. He was locking his mismatched eyes on Dom's.

Dom's own gaze was flitting from Yorak's icy blue to near black stare.

"You are going to let me in, Raze," Yorak said softly. "You feel safe with me. You love me. You can tell I am always helping you. Can't you?"

Yorak stroked the uninjured side of Dom's face.

"I'm going to let you rest here," the Wolf continued gently, "and when I say our secret words again, you'll remember me next time as the one who made you feel better."

It was almost shocking when the footage of such a seemingly tender scene melted into the next, which again started with a violent brawl.

This time Dom had been crossing the dusky road back to the diner – pinning a brooch to his t-shirt – when the camera, of course worn by a Hunter, charged him from behind.

A black stretch car pulled up, snatchers poured out, and Dom was engulfed before being thrown onto a leather seat – across Yorak's lap.

The camera clad Hunter and snatchers were incredibly fast at pouring back into the car, pinning Dom in place as the vehicle continued on its way.

And there was Rue, half visible, where she was wedged

between Dom's attackers. She was breathing hard, with wild eyes.

"What the f –"

Yorak placed a hand over Dom's lips. Then Dom's voice cut off more out of disgusted astonishment than anything else.

Dom glared up at Yorak furiously.

"It's new for you *every* time. But not for me," Yorak smiled down at Dom. "And I never tire of our time together. But I'll ask you again … Fight me? Or let me in, and save the child?"

Dom's confused eyes cut to the terrified Rue.

"Full disclosure," Yorak continued. "She's been betraying you. Pressing a little Wolf pager in her pocket when she sees you are alone. All I have to do is wait comfortably in my car for an hour or so of an evening."

Rue appeared ready to throw up.

"It's been *much* easier to slip into your head since you've actually come to know the little spy. Barely two weeks of loving her, and she can divert your focus beautifully."

Dom struggled against the Wolf's hold and the many snatcher hands.

"You're clearly choosing to fight. Does knowing everything mean her safety is not incentive enough to open your mind to me this time?" Yorak asked thoughtfully. "You see, what I'm doing isn't perfect or permanent. I need to learn what works for you. You'll need careful maintenance when you are finally ready to come with me."

Yorak seemed to recall an extra tidbit that might help then. "You might instead be relieved to know that I've decided on doing other things that might make you happy, in case you ever break free of my hold and need a reason to stay."

Dom said something unintelligible, yet clearly quite rude, against Yorak's hand.

"You can relax, knowing that the main thing I'm going to do," Yorak told him, peering down at Dom as if he had a lover laying in his lap. "Is ensure there is a code of conduct for buyers of any true Razes that are sold. It'll be like selling a puppy to only the nicest owners." He moved a loose flick of black hair back from Dom's forehead with his free hand. "Of course, if you ever leave me, I can take those puppies back and choose new owners. But hopefully you'll be grateful enough by then, if you wake from my fog."

Yorak took a moment to gaze into Dom's aggressive stare – checking for the right look in his fierce blue eyes.

"Hmm. No, you still seem rather closed off." He turned to Rue. "We'll go back to trying with you."

She squealed when a snatcher grabbed her wrist and yanked her closer to Dom, holding the back of her neck so she couldn't wriggle away, no matter how desperately she tried.

"Ouch, ouch!" she wailed. "You're hurting me!"

Dom's whole countenance changed. He slumped, going loose against his captors' grips, as if to say 'I'm listening!'

Yorak's face lit up.

"You want to fight it? Or let me in and save the child?" Yorak repeated.

He lifted his hand from Dom's lips.

Dom made an effort to talk steadily, with only steely hints of the terrible rage edging his words.

"Of course I choose the girl," he said slowly.

"Even if she keeps betraying you after this?" Yorak asked curiously. "You don't remember exactly what happens each time she leads you to me."

"I'll choose her every time," Dom gritted back.

Yorak nodded, as if he was finally seeing what he needed to see from Dom. "Good. Because I'm going to start to get her to be the one to administer your treatments between my visits. You won't need too much longer, and then one last big hit will do it."

"Nonono!" Rue keened when the snatchers forced Yorak's stun gun into her hand. She tried to bend her wrist every which way to get out of their hold as they pulled her close to Dom's head.

Yorak frowned at her in disapproval. "If you're not going to be useful …"

"It's alright Rue," Dom said more gently. "I think I remember this bit now."

He tried to relax for her sake. To show her he was fine.

"And I'll forgive you every time."

"Yes. That's how I need you!" Yorak quickly pressed Rue's fingers around the stunner, and she screamed as the shock aimed directly into Dom's skull made him strain and shake.

After five seconds, Rue was torn out of the way, and Yorak was stooping forward to whisper his words of control into Dom's ear.

The snatchers loosened their hold when Dom stirred – his hand shakily reaching to grip Yorak's jacket lapel, as if needing to hold something tangible and near.

Yorak hovered close, embracing Dom adoringly, with one hand over Dom's on the jacket lapel.

"You did so well to let me in, Raze," Yorak said softly. "You are safe with me. You love me. I am helping you."

Dom's gaze was flitting from Yorak's icy blue to near black eyes.

"You're ... the one who makes me feel better?"

"Yes. I am."

Dom was dazed as the car stopped in a street not too far away from the warehouse.

"Let me go too," Rue cried out when the snatchers opened the door. "Let me stay with him!"

"I think you're a bit too heightened, getting caught up in playing families, and might give our game away," Yorak answered. "For your sake, I hope you can keep up our treatment whenever he's alone. He'll need a little shock once a day before the last big dose."

"He'll get lost out there tonight," she said hysterically as Dom was lifted out of the car. "He's confused!"

"He's near his friends. They'll find him," Yorak said placidly. "Though there won't be many Razes left to bring him back to reality for long."

| 27 |

Twenty Seven

Sparks had rushed to the sink in the kitchen, retching.

Hato's fists were bunched.

Quicklips was shell-shocked.

"Flip's connection dropped out at the end," Jingle said dazedly, dashing tears from her face. "I can't get a response from them."

Pash stood abruptly – expression stony. "I have to go get Teddy. It's more dangerous than ever for any friends of our gang out there."

"Go," Hato rumbled at Quicklips. Who nodded, and pulled himself together to accompany Pash.

"I need check Dom," Frazzle said anxiously. He wanted to reassure himself.

Kiddo just blinked.

He was like a statue.

He wanted to join Sparks in retching over the sink, he wanted to punch a wall like Hato clearly wanted to, he was in shock like Quicklips, was ready to jump up and run like Pash, and … how were his cheeks dry while Jingle's weren't?

"Why would Yorak show us this?" Seethe hissed sickly. "Why bring us together for a 'family' viewing?"

Jingle was sniffling. Still trying to re-connect to the overseas Razes that had dropped out.

"They were in a hotel. They shouldn't have been cut off," she was muttering.

"Because he's messed up," Trix answered Seethe angrily.

"And our fire escape sensor was triggered while we were watching," Jingle went on under her breath, sniffing brusquely. "Those recruits better not have tripped something."

Ryo's phone was ringing and he stepped out of view on Trix's screen for a moment to answer, before hurriedly stepping back into the frame.

"Raze?" Ryo asked, his face pale.

Everyone froze.

"No, Raze, you haven't lived in Japan for a while now."

Blossom whirled to stare at Ryo.

Frazzle half fell down the steps in his rush to get back to the living level.

"Bedroom empty!" the doctor gasped. "Window open!"

"Raze you should go back to that room," Ryo was trying to sound calm. "No, it wasn't a snatcher place. Your gang are there." He listened worriedly. "I promise you do have a gang, you don't prefer to be alone anymore."

Ryo paused to take in what was being said.

"Just look at the fact that you actually have your own phone now, full of contacts. You were always so hard to reach before."

Ryo put a hand on Blossom's shoulder as he listened again.

"Blossom can't come to get you this time, you're too far away. Just head back to that base, and Kiddo will be there." Ryo swallowed, taking a steadying breath. "Kiddo ... well, he's your partner ... Don't hang up!"

Ryo stared at his phone in dismay.

There was a thump from the kitchen as Sparks slumped to the floor in a faint.

Frazzle dashed to her at once, but she was already coming around – simply as overwhelmed as Kiddo felt.

Kiddo stood. "Seethe and Hato, help me find him," he said in a numb voice.

"Raze described where he wanted Blossom to go," Ryo told them quickly. "He didn't know where he was, but he said he could see water in the distance."

"He's headed to the docks," Seethe stated.

Jingle crossed to Sparks, helping the mechanic into a chair. "Frazzle, go check on things at the clinic. Stay with Daleeah."

"When we find Dom, we'll bring him straight in to you," Hato affirmed.

Kiddo only paused to kiss Sparks' forehead, before Seethe and Hato flanked him down the stairs.

| 28 |

Twenty Eight

"Be on alert," Hato told the recruits in the training area. He didn't mind that Madam Hellion and Sora heard him. "The Wolf is playing with us. Something might be going on."

Then Seethe, Kiddo and Hato were revving their bikes to life and ducking under the still ascending roller door.

They flew through the night, eyes scanning the streets that led to the docks.

They only slowed as they got to the road that curved around the coastline.

If Dom's memory had blurred, he would not recognise the remodelled commercial hub that had grown around the water after the capital's snatcher base had been destroyed by the Raze gang.

He would be disoriented.

Where might he unconsciously be drawn to go?

Kiddo moved up to take the lead, spearheading the three bikes as they cruised.

He couldn't help but push up the pace, heading for the far

side of the water, where there had once been old wire fencing and a pile of dumped concrete cylinders.

It was where he had hidden Dom, again after a head injury, when Dom had first saved Kiddo from getting snatched.

Now it was a well-lit outlook, surrounded in open grass and pavement. Dom and Kiddo's hiding place had been taken over by a merry-go-round that filled the area with music and drew children in crowds by day.

Kiddo's heart raced as they drew closer.

There was a lone figure, wandering listlessly through the still horses of the darkened carousel.

Wearing blue jeans and a white t-shirt, and lacking his trademark leather – in spite of the cold.

Kiddo dragged to a stop, tearing up luscious new lawn, and practically threw himself off the bike.

He dropped his helmet even as Dom was whirling around to see what new danger had come upon him.

Hato and Seethe quickly pulled up on either side of Kid.

"Go slow," Hato intoned a caution. "Don't spook him."

"Who the hell are you?" Dom yelled, in no way appearing at risk of bolting from their perceived threat.

Instead, he dropped down from the carousel, arms slightly out from his body. Wired for action.

Even the light footed, yet wide steps he took toward them suggested he was ready to fight his way out of something.

"Uh oh," Seethe breathed.

Kiddo had never been the *target* of this side of Dom before.

His blue eyes were blazing.

"I saaaid, who the *hell* are you?"

Dom came to a stop on the grass a short distance away.

"You the ones who had me in that building? Why'd you take me out of Tokyo?"

Hato raised his hands in a placating manner, but Dom's stance lowered ever so marginally in readiness – as if the big man had raised his fists.

"Dominic, you know me," Hato said slowly. "I am Hato, and you remember Seethe."

This time it was as if Hato had actually landed punches. Right to the heart.

Dom's middle sucked in with a hissed intake of breath and his face went from heated defensiveness to stone.

"I haven't seen them since I was eight," Dom said in a dangerous voice. "You think you can use their names to trick me? They don't remember I exist."

Seethe cocked his head to the side. "Come on Dom, Hato's a whole lot bigger, but I sorta look the same, right?"

Kiddo noticed both Hato and Seethe taking small steps closer, subtly trying to come in on either side of Dom.

"I don't know you," Dom stated icily. "It would be smart to leave me alone."

Kiddo tried now. "Dom, were you surprised not to find a pipe here? It was our hiding place. I think you were searching for it."

Dom blanched – as if hit with an invisible blow to the skull, to go with the bruises to the heart.

"And who are you then? The one Hato and Seethe replaced me with?"

This time it wasn't just Kiddo who noticed Hato and Seethe making slight moves to close Dom in.

Dom flexed his fingers and gave them a devilish grin.

"I *warned* you."

Seethe made to pounce, but Dom jabbed a fast fist into Seethe's side – ploughing forward at the same time to charge Seethe with his shoulder.

Seethe went soaring backward, landing lithely, but clutching his ribs.

Dom was already elbowing Kiddo in the face.

And though Hato rushed forward to get his arms around Dom in a trap-like hold, Dom immediately jabbed at Hato's front and slipped free – as fast as a piece of soap shooting out of wet, desperate hands.

He struck upward at Hato's wide chin, put a boot on Hato's knee, made an agile step up, and launched himself high enough to land a blow against Hato's thick neck.

Hato keeled over at once, his legs crumpling.

Blinking stars from his eyes, Kiddo darted in again, but Dom struck Kiddo in the stomach with a fist that moved so fast it was like a snake striking.

With a tap on Kiddo's neck, pins and needles shot down his lower half and he found himself collapsing too.

Dom gave Seethe a wicked smile as he caught Seethe circling around him again.

They simultaneously launched at each other, and somehow Dom had Seethe on the ground in seconds. A tattooed arm had Seethe in a chokehold, and Dom's fingers were just searching for a dangerous place to pinch on Seethe's neck, when the headlights of a car dazzled his eyes.

He squinted as the black stretch pulled up in a smooth park alongside them.

Instead of a death stroke, Seethe was dropped to the grass, gasping for air, and Dom was staring at the man who was stepping from the vehicle.

"Dom," Kiddo gaped, scrabbling to try to get some feeling flowing through his legs. Fighting to pull himself closer.

"Raze, they are not lying," the Wolf said. "That is Seethe and Hato."

Even Seethe paused in sucking in breaths, to stare in surprise.

"It is as you feared. They were changed by the snatchers. They are terrorists. Come away from them."

The Wolf held out a hand to beckon Dom over.

Dom's face had become puzzled instead of murderous.

"I know you from somewhere," Dom said, as if surfacing from a bad dream. "You've been there, and helped me … when I wasn't well. They must have done something to me … but you made me feel better."

"That's right Raze," Yorak nodded. "I was there for you each time you felt worst." His face was so earnest. "I found you, and you're safe with me. You love me. I am always helping you."

Dom's whole body relaxed. The fight went out of him.

Kiddo tried to make a grab for Dom's ankle, and Hato was attempting valiantly to rise.

But Dom stepped past them, shaking his head in relief.

"Yorak?" Dom said. "Your name is Yorak Wolf? I ... remember that."

Yorak smiled so radiantly. "Yes, that's it. You know me."

"Dom, don't listen to him, please," Kiddo tried to drag himself along the grass. It was as if Dom had administered an epidural. Half his body was heavier than lead. But if he could get the blood flowing, it would pass. He just had to hurry up!

Dom was rubbing his brow, and he shook his head a couple more times, as if to clear it.

He moved more purposefully toward Yorak now.

"Yorak ... do you think I could go with you?" Dom asked plaintively. "I don't think I'm well right now either."

He made it to Yorak's waiting arms, and half crumpled when he got there. As if it was all too much.

Yorak caught him easily, sweeping his form around to lean him up against the car.

"You want to stay with me?" Yorak asked kindly. "You're choosing to stay with me?"

Dom gripped Yorak's shirt as an anchor while the Wolf held him up. He couldn't seem to settle his gaze on either of Yorak's mismatched eyes.

"Yes, can I?" Dom asked. He grimaced with a pained expression. "I think I need you."

Yorak leaned forward, as if he were going to take a stolen kiss from Dom. But instead he whispered something in Dom's ear.

Dom sagged, letting his head drop to Yorak's shoulder. "Thank you."

The Wolf cast a single gaze back at the three stricken Razes on the grass. His eyes were on Kiddo.

"I'll take good care of you, Raze," Yorak promised. And he lowered Dom into the car.

| 29 |

Twenty Nine

"That didn't just happen ..." Kiddo was rambling. "That didn't just happen ..."

Seethe was the first to recover, holding his throat and wincing at the agony of his ribs.

He stumbled across to Hato, who was close to standing.

"Dominic is a dangerous enemy to have," Hato said hollowly. "But, if he wanted us dead, we would be dead. He might unconsciously have held back."

"Oh, I don't doubt I would be dead and you two would have been next if Yorak hadn't swept in," Seethe stated. His cheek was swelling and there was blood on his teeth. "I never expected it to go like that."

"Hato," Kiddo said desperately, wobbling up into a kneeling position. "Call the others. Get the patrol bikes out after that car. We can force him to come back with us and work out a solution with Frazzle."

Seethe, favouring his left side, had just helped Hato to prop himself up on his feet. But when Hato opened his phone, the big man staggered again.

"What?" Kiddo panicked. "What is it?"

Hato had clapped a giant hand to his mouth, and he sank all the way back down.

"Oh shit …" Seethe was reading over Hato's shoulder. "Oh … shit …"

Kiddo wrestled his own phone from his pocket and fumbled to unlock it.

The group chat opened to a stream of messages, and he had to scroll rapidly upward to work it out.

Jingle had messaged when they'd left.

Jingle: I'm worried. I can't get onto Flip's team or any of their graduates.

Jingle: guys, they're not just offline. It's like their devices don't exist anymore.

Ten minutes had passed before anyone had messaged back in the chat.

And the next one made Kiddo's heart stop.

Quicklips: … Hurt. Car run off. Teddy bad. Pash bad.

Quicklips: They're coming. Can't get out.

Jingle: Quicklips, where are you?

Jingle: Quicklips?

There was a gap of another ten minutes.

Trix: Jingle, did you hear anything? What's going on?

Jingle: Sora and the recruits said vans are pulling up outside.

Sparks: going to check cabinets are safe.

Jingle: I'll lock down my tech.

Trix: Sparks, Jingle, get out of there.

Jingle: oh my God. I can see fire from my window.

Jingle: Kid's Place is on fire. Oh my God.

Sparks: Jingle. Safe room! They're here!

Five minutes.

Trix: Sparks? Jingle?

Jingle: there's fighting down below.

Jingle: Sparks? Quicklips? Flip? Hato? ... Trix, I'm panicking.

Trix: hide. You need to hide.

Jingle: I'm in the library safe room.

Trix: it's alright, stay nice and quiet.

Jingle: There are footsteps on the stairs.

Jingle: I love you. I love my family.

Jingle: they're right outside the door.

Trix: Jingle?

Trix: Jingle, please answer.

Trix: is there nobody left?

Trix: Jingle..?

RECEIVE YOUR EXTRA RAZE WARFARE CHAPTER WHEN YOU SIGN UP FOR SHELLEY CASS' VIP LIST. GET YOUR BONUS HERE:

VIP Reader Gift:

https://www.shelleycass.com/coming-soon-02

OTHER BOOKS BY SHELLEY CASS

The Raze Warfare Series

'A Fairy's Tale' Epic Fantasy Series:
Book One – 'The Last Larnaeradee'
Book Two – 'The Raiden'
Book Three – 'The Army for the World'

Dystopian Future:
'Awaken Dreamer'

Contemporary/Action/Fantasy/Erotica:
'Darkling'

The Sleep Sweet Series for children:
Book One – 'Little Pixie's Christmas'
Book Two – 'The case of the bored baby Ace'
Book Three – 'Mum and Me'
Book Four – 'The Cloud and the Flower'
Book Five – 'Hush'

Dear reader,
I would love to hear from you!
Please leave a review and feel free to visit my author
Facebook page or website shelleycass.com

ACKNOWLEDGMENTS

I am so thankful for the friends who understand me and embrace who I am.

I am so appreciative of my work family, for being my silver lining even on the most stressful days.

I am so appreciative of Wendy – the greatest neighbour to have ever lived, and Linda – the greatest mother to have ever lived. Your patience with reading my novels when they are still rough, clunky, colossal things is indescribably helpful.

I am so grateful for an extended family of extensive love: the bubbly and boisterous Brittinghams, Burkes and Rigbys, and the gracious, gorgeous Tangees, Lennens and Plants. My grandparents too, though lost, are such a special part of me.

I am so thankful for Linda (mum) and Robert (dad), who would move heaven and earth to make us happy.

For my sisters and best friends, Melissa and Leigh.

For my brother in law, Andrew, and the lights of my life – Jack and Elyssia.

For the love of my life, my sunshine, Jarryd.

And for the little year eight version of me, who first picked up that pen to write.

ABOUT THE AUTHOR

I was an awkward, reserved year 8 – totally in love with the escape offered by the novels I read. I could hear the voices of the authors' characters, I could tune out my stresses and uncertainties as I journeyed with each protagonist through their own troubles. And then one day I could hear the voices of characters who hadn't been written yet, in places that hadn't been created, and I decided to write my own worlds.

In the real world I became a high school teacher, and still face the epic battle of staying afloat in all the papers I must assess. And in the real world the magic has also sometimes been hard to find. Stress and disunity surface like cancer – making the nightly news too hard to watch on most days.

But in the real world there has also been inspiration – incredible students, loved ones, golden memories, growing up, warm hugs, big laughs and good people.

One of the greatest things achieved in my lifetime that I can remember, and that had a profound impact on me, was when Australia legalised equal marriage. I'd had this terrible sick fear that it wouldn't happen, and that I would have to face the fact that a majority of the people in my country do not want progress or equality. I would have to face the fact that some of my students and friends would not have the same rights or access to a future that I could choose to have. Teaching teens to reach for their dreams in a climate like that just seemed too hopeless. But instead, I remember sitting next to mum – happy tears streaming down her face – as something incredibly good was achieved. We proved that the majority of people appreciate love and the right to love in all forms. That love is love. Which is damn important in a world that can be so harsh.

So I wrote of the things that threaten the world, and of the big and small things that save it. I wish for a real world where the air is clean, the trees can grow without concrete borders, the darkness can be cured with the switch of a light, and the people can all have long days and happy lives.